This version dedicated to Father John Gerard, S.J.

ISBN 978-1-304-97952-0

Written by ear

from the audio edition recorded by Maria Therese

Formatted, typed, and edited by Eliza Quille and Maria Farmer

Murder in the Sacristy

By Daniel A. Lord, S.J.

Chapter One

It was exactly 8:15 when I mounted the stairs to the little choir loft, each ancient step squeaking under my none-too-dainty shoes. The light over the organ had been turned on. A low purr from the organ indicated that the motor was running, and the pump heaving expectantly. But Karl Reinhardt wasn't there, though on the music rack was the music manuscript that he always dragged around with him whenever he thought he might have a few spare minutes at the keyboard. That's the way young composers are, you know.

The body of the little church was dark. In spite of all the work that Father Mark Tierney had done on it during the past two weeks, it still looked far more Protestant than Greek Uniate. After all, you can't convert an old Protestant church into one of the Oriental Rite of the Catholic Church, with a few strokes of a paint brush and the addition of a Greek altar and the essential icons. Still, with Father Tierney in his new Greek vestments, Karl at the organ, and myself singing the beautiful, if melancholy, responses of the liturgy, the church when it was officially opened on the coming Sunday, probably wouldn't displease the few Greeks and White Russians who made up it's sketchy membership.

I moved about the organ loft briefly, and sat down on the organ bench and improvised a few chords. I'm not much of an organist, but I managed a handful or so of fairly matched notes when the old wheezy organ emitted a squeak. I stopped and turned around, wondering just what had happened to Karl. For it was all a little queer; the lights on, the organ motor running, music set on the rack, the church dark, and no Karl. He was such a thoroughly reliable fellow, but if he set the time of rehearsal at 8:15, nothing would keep him away but an accident; a sudden death; a murder.

I heard the door of the sacristy bang open with a vicious thump. A flash of light spread into the reconstructed sanctuary. Karl leaped out into the light, and looked up toward the organ loft. The church was not long, and it didn't take much scrutiny to realize that Karl was in some wild mood. He yelled, "Pierre!"

I answered across the empty church.

"It's murder!" he cried. "Come down as fast as you can."

Murder! I dashed across the organ loft, switching off the organ motor as I ran, clattered down the narrow, resounding stairs and through the church with it's scarred old pews, now faintly lighted from the sacristy, and ploughed into the chancel. Karl grabbed my shoulder and pushed me forward, at the same time restraining me in my mad rush from going far enough to fall over what lay stretched out on the floor of the sacristy. It was the Russian sacristan, Ivan Radolf. His body had fallen forward, away from the sanctuary, and his face had turned as he fell, so that now it was in profile on the dark rug.

I knelt at his side in an impulsive movement that was mostly curiosity. His body was still warm, but the back of his head had been bashed in with a blow that clearly had squashed out any possible speck of life. I got to my feet slowly.

"No doubt about it," I said; "He's dead. But even so, there's a chance, and if we phone at once for the police and the doctor…"

Karl's strong hand, the hand of a skillful musician, swung me around, and I saw what he meant me to see. In the wall of the reconstructed sacristy, which had once been the plain little vestry of the old Protestant church, Father Tierney had built a small wall-safe. The safe's door had been wrenched open and it hung crazily, like a broken gate, from the wall. I peered inside, even though there was light enough to make close scrutiny unnecessary. It was stripped clean.

"Had Father Tierney used that to store anything?" I asked.

"Had he!" replied Karl.

We stood there looking at each other, the dead man lying between us. I don't know what that strange paralysis is that comes over all men in the presence of death, and far more stranglingly in the presence of death by murder. I just know that for a moment neither of us wanted to move.

It was Karl who broke the paralysis. Karl is a natural leader, and he takes situations in hand.

"We'll get Father Tierney," he said quietly. "At the same time we can call the police. Will you stay with the body?"

"Let *me* go," I said, "And *you* stay here till we come back."

Despite the situation Karl grinned. He reached over the dead man and patted my arm. "We'll both go," he said, "Come on."

And he circled the body swiftly and made for the sacristy's rear door which gave on the small yard, the alley, and a short cut to the rectory. I followed him but stopped when Karl's strong hand grabbed the handle, fumbled for the key, rattled and shook the door. He turned back, puzzled.

"It's locked" he said in explanation, "And the key's gone."

He lifted his hand and even with the shadow of the door knob falling upon it, I could see that the keyhole was empty. We stood again with that same hesitancy.

I wondered whether Karl thought he saw doubt or suspicion in my eyes, for he hurried into a quick explanation. "I came in just a little earlier than I'd expected," he said. "Tonight during dinner the first notes of a melody started stringing themselves together in my mind and I knew that if I could get a few minutes at a keyboard…so I dropped into the church using my front door key, of course. It was just about 8:00." He stopped and thought, puckered his forehead. "It must have been slightly after 8:00, for when I stopped in the drug store for a package of cigarettes the clock, I remember, showed not quite 8:00. I turned on the light, started the motor, and sat down to try out the melody. You know how it is when a fellow has an idea and wants to get it down on paper.

"I was all wrapped up in it, but not so wrapped up that I didn't hear some sort of a muffled sound from the sacristy—that is, I thought it came from the sacristy. But my stars! With the noises on Blue Island Avenue, cars, motors, wagons, kids shouting, well I wasn't sure, and so I went on playing.

"Then I did hear something. It was the sound of a door opening and closing. Then there was just one muffled groan and a thump. You know that unmistakable thump of a body falling heavily, in a faint, in death. I know that I stopped playing and sat there on the bench, wondering whether I was getting the jitters or whether I had heard something I should investigate.

"Pierre, that's where I made my mistake. If I had moved the second I heard that thump I might have caught the murderer."

His hand moved toward the body in a sort of sick revulsion. I put my fingers reassuringly on his arm.

"And maybe got a blow or a bullet that would've piled you right on top of him." I said. "No, thank God you didn't rush right down into a murderer's arms. Then what?"

"Well, I finally decided to investigate. I just couldn't go back to my keyboard with that thump reverberating in my mind, so I walked quietly down the stairs and made my way on tip-toe through the dark church, opened the sacristy door quietly and, I don't know why, closed it behind me.

"I had the deuce of a time finding that switch. This makeshift church doesn't even have electric switches where anyone can find them. But because I was searching for the switch I moved around the walls, almost hugging them, and that kept me from falling over the body; though all the time—I give you my word, Pierre, it was a ghastly feeling—I knew that there was another human being in that little room, and that something was terribly wrong with him.

"I found the switch over there." He pointed to its place near the locked door that lead out of the sacristy to the small yard and alley beyond. "I snapped it on and, well, then I bolted for the sanctuary door, flung it open, saw you and called."

"Steady, lad." I said, tightening my grip on his arm. "The police will have this all in hand in no time, and we'll probably be back at our rehearsal inside an hour."

"Poor Father Mark!" he said. "All set to open his little church next Sunday. Come on." And we hurried back through the dimly lighted church, out the doorway and onto Blue Island Avenue, and then to the little cottage next door, which Father Mark Tierney was using as an improvised rectory. Everything about St. Sergius' Greek Uniate Church, as you certainly guessed by this time, was pretty much improvised. I'm afraid we pushed that bell with an emphasis and insistence frowned on by any book of etiquette, but it brought Father Tierney to the door in a hurry, and he grinned at us in that friendly Irish fashion of his.

"Hi boys," he said, "and how's the greatest choir in the length and breadth of the archdiocese of Chicago tonight?"

"Father Mark," said Karl, breathlessly, "something terrible's happened! Come along over to the church."

I'll give Father Mark full credit; he's the kind that wastes no words when the situation calls for movement. He literally pushed us back off the little step that lead us to his cottage, onto the sidewalk and then, grabbing each of us by an arm, propelled us toward the church. He didn't say a word, but once inside the church he stopped and Karl took the lead.

"This way," said Karl, and we moved up the aisle with very unritualistic haste and scrambling. I stood watching Father Tierney as he stopped in the doorway of the sacristy and saw the murdered man.

"Ivan!" he said, and then turned to take over the situation. "Karl, stay here with me. Pierre, dash over to the house and call for the police. Tell them to bring a doctor or get one yourself if you can. I'll give the poor fellow conditional absolution and conditional Extreme Unction. Quick!" And then his eyes lifted from the man on the floor to the open wall safe, its door wrenched loose and hanging clumsily against the newly papered wall. He stood looking at it for a second as if he couldn't bring himself to believe what he saw.

When he turned toward us, (we were standing behind him and halfway in the sanctuary) his face was the color of fresh dough, his eyes were dark with incredulous anguish. "Was that," he managed to say, though you could tell his tongue was dry and unmanageable, "Was that, *that* way when you found him?" Karl nodded. I looked at Father and followed his gaze.

"What's gone?" I demanded, "What's missing?" There was something close to hysteria in the laughter that took him by the throat and shook him briefly. "What's missing!" he echoed, "Nothing! Oh, oh nothing but the sacred vessels for Sunday mass—unconsecrated as yet." he added, the priest speaking over the voice of an obviously stricken man. I sighed in audible relief.

"That's bad." I consoled him, "but, after all, you have friends. They'll be glad to replace the sacred vessels; you can borrow others for the time being, and since they were not consecrated—"

Father Mark looked at me as if I were a lunatic mumbling some atrocious nonsense, pushed by me and hurried to the back of the altar where I heard him open a little door that contained, I suppose, the elements he meant to use for the fallen man. Since I myself am not a Catholic, either of the Greek or the Latin rite, it was all a little mysterious and unintelligible to me. I turned to Karl. "What's wrong?" I demanded. "Why is he so cut up about a few cheap altar vessels?"

Karl looked at me almost pityingly. "Because, you poor fool, in those altar vessels have been placed a fortune in jewels; the priceless collection of the Countess Olga Stefanska. That's why." I know I whistled. The news should have added speed to my feet as I ploughed out of the church once more, hit the cement side walk, brushed aside a couple of men dressed in some uniform that vaguely suggested German storm troopers, flung open the door of the little rectory and jammed the receiver of the priest's phone against my ear.

I don't know just how I phrased it to the officer who answered to my call but I remember I managed the words "murder" and "jewel theft" and I know that his tone leaped from resentment to electric interest. I stood at the door of the little church as the squad car came shrieking up and the children of the neighborhood crowded around in suddenly awakened interest. It seemed to me that another car was right on its heels, and then came a couple of motorcycles that ejected more police. I led the police down the aisle, reaching the sacristy just as Father Mark was rising to his feet and taking off some sort of small garment he was wearing. The policeman who had reached the scene first glared first at the murdered man, then at the open safe, then at Father Mark.

"You haven't touched anything?" He demanded. "Just enough to give the man the Last Sacraments." said the priest. And then suddenly the little sacristy and the sanctuary beyond seemed to pop open with the mass of cops that filled it. I know for the next few minutes we heard questions that nobody seemed to answer, and answered questions that nobody seemed to have asked. The little church was teeming with reporters and photographers and more policemen and wild confusion, and loud talking; and then police photographers and a coroner.

And then, mercifully, young detective Sergeant Art Reilly. Up to that time we felt as if we were the center of a motion picture climax in which the director had mixed tragedy with the wildest slapstick comedy; drama with utter farce. But Sergeant Reilly took over and we sighed with relief. He started by bodily throwing everybody out of the sacristy except what was still a sizable assembly; Father Tierney, Karl, myself and one policeman—the particular squad cop who had arrived first on the scene.

"Search the place from top to bottom," he ordered the other policeman, "and clear out everybody that's not official. When you finish that, search the surroundings. It's possible that whatever they took—well, they may have dropped some of it, lost it. Anyhow, get out of my way until I send for you." And they cleared. We stood with our backs against the wall. Sergeant Reilly and the officer stood on the far side where they could face the safe and the small vesting table, and the murdered man was lying like a barrier between us. We three, the priest, the organist and myself, leaned against the vesting table and answered questions.

First Karl told his story almost in the exact words in which he had told it to me. Clearly the events of the evening had cut a groove in his brain and I imagined idly that whenever henceforth he told the story (which would probably be plenty often,) he'd tell it in exactly those same words. Then the sergeant shifted to Father Mark.

"Well Father," he said in a tone that showed he was not merely a Catholic, but probably a good one, "tell me once more just what's missing and how you happened to have the stuff." Father Tierney took a deep breath. "I've been living in my little rectory you know, hardly more then two weeks, until the church could be got ready. I've been saying my Mass in the little convent over on 13th Street. Well the very day after I took over the church and the rectory this strange lady called on me. You could tell she was a lady even though she was dressed poorly. She told me she was working as some sort of receptionist in a department store restaurant."

Sgt. Reilly made a quick note, asked the name of the department store and then the name of the women.

"She's calling herself Erma Romani," the priest answered quickly.

"Calling herself?" The detective looked up in quick suspicion.

I could see Father Tierney hesitate. "I don't know whether I have the right," he said, "to tell her name."

Reilly took a step toward the door, swung it open and looked out. The police were combing the church with practiced skill, but none of them were near the door of the sacristy except the patrolman who stood on guard.

Reilly closed the door quietly. "You have to tell, Father," he said. "And there are just us here to know about it until I see the woman myself."

"She's really the Countess Olga Stefanska," he said. "I told my friend Karl here because I wanted to talk it over with someone. Sargeant, I've been an awful fool about this, I'm afraid."

"Go on," said the sergeant, who had, one could tell, met plenty of bigger fools in his day. "What does she want with you?"

"She brought the most magnificent display of unset jewels I had ever seen in my life. She poured them out on the little table in my rectory, and I must have blinked, for she smiled and said, 'Father, when my family escaped the murderous Reds this is all that they took with them. These jewels are all that remain of what was once one of the great fortunes of the Russian nobility. I've never sold one. Never pawned one. I'm keeping them—and I remember that she set her jaw so that highlights settled in the tight lines of her cheek—till the day when the stench of the Soviet is gone from Russia and I can return, regain my lands and live as a Russian noblewoman should. "

The sergeant went briefly cynical. "A lady with a nice sense of the dramatic," he said. Then to the priest, "Go on, Father, if you will."

"Well," the priest continued, taking another deep breath, "She put it this way, 'If it becomes known that I have these jewels, there are a thousand men who would kill me willingly to get them.' "

Again the sergeant interrupted. "Did she mention any of them?" he demanded. "Any, that is, by name?"

The priest shook his head. "She somehow seemed to expect me to understand what she meant. Well, she finally got to her point. 'Father,' she said, 'the safest possible place for these jewels would be in the sacred vessels. No one would dream of looking for them there. Besides,' and she smiled shyly, 'I am myself a Uniate Catholic, and though I could not give even to the Lord my family's fortune, I should like for a time to have these jewels serve Him. I suppose a million crimes have been committed because of them. Maybe for a little while they can be devoted to Christ and his Church.' "

The sergeant looked at the priest, his eyebrows knitted, his head tilted far forward. "So the jewels were merely a loan to be returned? When?"

"I don't know," the priest replied.

"How many of them? What proportion have been used for the sacred vessels?"

"I wanted speed, for I'm opening—or I *was* opening—our little church on Sunday. So I took them to Goldleaves, a highly respected, very conservative firm, as you know, and asked them to take care of the assignment at once. Today they returned to me a chalice, two ciboria, and the remaining unset jewels. Almost half of the lot. I put them all in the wall safe just before dinner, and now…"

I thought for a moment that he was going to break down, but the sergeant cut in, walked across the rear door of the sacristy and laid his hand on the knob. "I'm taking a look around and back," he said. "Obviously, since Mr. Reinhardt, and later Mr. Anton here, were out in the church the murderer went this way."

He rattled the knob and it held. He fumbled for the key and found none.

I noticed that Fr. Tierney had moved out into the sanctuary and was kneeling before an icon, on which the light from the sacristy shone brightly.

"The door is locked," said the sergeant, puzzling over the obvious.

Karl spoke up. "The janitor here, Ivan, would have the key."

The sergeant was on his knees beside the dead man and going through his pockets. He brought forth a bundle of keys and tried each of them. None of them fitted.

"Strange," mused Reilly, aloud. "None of them works, yet he should have had..." He went to the sanctuary door and called Fr.

Tierney in a low voice. "Sorry, Father, but have you a key to the sacristy door?"

Fr. Tierney dug inside his cassock and pulled out a bunch of keys, selected one and handed it to the sergeant. The detective took it, but instead of going to the door, stood holding it in his hand and regarding it with a speculative eye.

Swiftly he turned on the priest. "How does it happen that this man, who is both a janitor and a sacristan, had no key to the sacristy?" he demanded sharply.

The priest looked up, puzzled. "But he had a key," he answered. "I gave it to him when he took over last week."

"I'm sorry," said the detective, "but he hasn't any sign of that key tonight. Who else, besides yourself and the sacristan, has a key to the sacristy?"

"No one," replied the priest.

Karl interfered. "After all," he said, "this was until recently a Protestant church and any of a dozen men might have kept keys for the vestry."

I stumbled in, and I realized that I stumbled even as I spoke. "But Fr. Tierney had the lock on that door changed, don't you remember?" It was a bad blunder and I know I flushed as I spoke. I hadn't realized what might be implied in the fact that Fr. Tierney had the only key to the sacristy that we could find, and the sacristan had none.

"Unless," said the sergeant, almost as if he were reading my mind, "the sacristan here gave his key to some one."

A patrolman appeared in the doorway. "They've come for the body," he said, and we all stepped back against the wall, while the newly arrived squad came in. With practiced callousness they picked up the body of the murdered man and carried it out through the narrow doorway.

The eyes of all of us followed the grim procession; death at it's ugliest, and then, as we heard the footsteps resounding through the little church, our eyes swung back. Almost simultaneously we seemed to see the object on the floor, but the sergeant swung into action first. There, crushed by the body of the dead sacristan, was a small piece of black cloth, shapeless and indistinguishable. But I'm sure there was not a man in the room who did not realize what it was, even before Sgt. Reilly's deft fingers had shaped it back from its original form.

It was a priest's biretta that immerged from the battered piece of cloth that had been crushed by the body of the murdered man. And when the detective turned it over, the light of the sacristy lamps seemed to pick out with fiendish delight the initials on the inside: M.T., they read. And every eye swung involuntarily and fastened upon the white faced young priest.

Chapter Two

We stood, the lot of us facing Fr. Tierney with something close to horror on our faces. I could see the web of circumstantial evidence that already was fastening around him: he was a poor young priest, the custodian of jewels that he would someday have to relinquish; he was the only one who had a key for that rear sacristy door through which the murderer had clearly passed; his biretta had been crushed by the falling body of the Russian sacristan, who had evidently interrupted the thief removing the precious stones. Yet it was all so absurd. Karl and I looked at each other, and except for the stark horror of the moment, I could see that Karl wanted to laugh—laugh at the whole absurdity of the thing.

But before I go on, it is only decent to explain how an Irish-American boy, and American of German extraction and a Polish singer should have been thrown together in the setting of a Greek Uniate church. And that necessitates a brief journey that takes us back to the deck of an ocean liner bound from Le Havre to New York.

I had finished my musical training in the Paris Conservatory. Nature (and God, if you want to use the term) had given me a better than ordinary baritone voice. An opportunity had made possible a year of training under the great singing teachers that gather in Paris the way brokers gather in Wall Street. On the ship coming back with me was Karl Reinhardt, who, though we had never met, had been studying piano and composition for three years in Paris, played marvelously and ran off for me a few little things of his own that someday the better type records will be offering to collectors and that great conductors will gladly include in their programs.

We had been swimming in the ship's pool and were tossing the ring across the deck tennis net when we noticed a young fellow come out, slip off a dressing gown, dive neatly into the pool, swim across it's narrow width with two powerful strokes, laze about in the water and then climb out to watch us with a friendly grin. We, with a careless camaraderie of ship ward, invited him into the game; and to our amazement, he beat us individually, and then took us both on and trimmed the two of us together. It wasn't until that evening when he appeared in the dining salon wearing a Roman collar that I knew he was a priest. And it wasn't until we had come to be good friends that he told us the really interesting things about himself: that he was a Brooklyn lad who had volunteered for the Russian mission; that he completed his seminary days and had been ordained in the pope's own Russian college in Rome, and that, until the day came when he could slip past the guards who turned back all priests from Russian soil, he'd accepted the opportunity of working among the Russians and Greeks of Chicago.

"That will make me letter perfect in the ritual, in the language, and if you think it doesn't take a bit of rustling to get my Irish tongue around that language and those tunes, you have three more guesses coming. But one of these days," he added, and there was a light in his eyes as he said it, "I'll be getting into Russia and helping to bring back the Church and Christ to that sad, sad land."

He was a persuasive chap, no doubt of that, and though I am not, as I've said, a Catholic, and Karl during his days in Paris hadn't spent too much time on his knees, that young Irish-Russian-Greek persuaded us to help him out with his new parish. So Karl agreed to play the organ for him. Truth to tell, I think he was delighted with the chance to soak up that marvelous musical ocean—that is, the Greek liturgy—and the first thing I knew, I said I'd sing for him, being the only member of his choir.

If we thought that was all we'd have to do for Fr. Mark, we were badly fooled. He dragged us around Chicago until we located this little Protestant church, which was standing idle and going to decay on the Westside's polyglot, Blue Island Avenue. Once it had served as a sort of chapel for the Hallstead Social Center down the street, but since the Italians didn't take much to Protestant services, and the clinic at the Center cut down the population and its own clientele by generous lessons in birth control, the chapel had fallen into disuse. So Fr. Mark had the two of us wrangling the real estate agents to let him have it for nothing down and a little each year. The miracle is that he got it and faced the future of his as yet nonexistent congregation with absolute confidence.

"They'll come," he bragged happily, "what with my magnificent basso in the Mass, Karl's handling of that wheezy box he calls his organ, and Pierre's bountiful baritone we'll have them hanging from the rafters…if we ever happen to have rafters."

Ivan Radolf he had picked up at the House of Hospitality of the Catholic workers down the street. He chose him simply because he was a Russian, looked hungry, and talked himself eloquently into the job of sacristan and janitor. Personally I think Radolf had never had a broom in his hand and I saw him use the claw end of a hammer to drive a nail. But Fr. Mark swore by his find and bragged that he was probably a great nobleman.

"We may not have much of an edifice," he said, "but it's something to have a janitor who once, I'm sure of it, held the imperial boot tree for Tsar Nicholas of all the Russias."

Not that Ivan ever proclaimed to be anything more than the bum Karl and I had pronounced him. But it was Fr. Mark's pet joke and we let it go at that.

The jewels? Well, for some reason he had told Karl about them. I'm not going to be jealous over the fact that he kept them a secret from me. It was clear that he liked Karl the better of the two of us, which seemed natural enough; since Karl's a charming fellow and a Catholic to boot and few people would class me as either. So that explains how we stood there in the sudden realization that we had to line up shoulder to shoulder in the face of this horrible crime. Suspicion had fallen like the blow of a heavy hand on the shoulder of our young priest friend.

I'll say this for Sgt. Reilly; I've never seen a police officer that had a clue right in his hands, who looked unhappier than he did. He turned that funny shaped biretta over and over in his fingers and said not a word. Finally, drawing himself together with visible effort, he held it out toward the priest. "This, Father," he said, and all his Catholic instincts resented the question he had to ask, "is obviously yours."

The priest nodded dumbly.

Well, I thought, *innocent men usually look most guilty. They have no prepared alibis, no glib explanations.*

"Can you explain how it happened to be...on the floor, under the body of the murdered man?" Fr. Mark shook his head. "I'm a pretty careless sort of fellow, Sergeant," he said, his face alternately pale as death and flushed with a guilty colour. "But I know positively, I've never worn that into the church. I hate anything on my head.

The Sisters keep a biretta for me in their chapel; I'd almost forgotten I had another one."

"But you did have one," said the police officer. "And this is yours?"

He nodded sadly.

Then across the silence cut the sudden sound of men's voices in song. I remember that the music came with a kind of savage beauty. Rugged, untrained voices shot through with emotional depth and the white heat of fierce passion. It wasn't like the music of some college glee club or a mere choral society that was practicing a favourite quartette arrangement. It was set to the tempo of boots beating on a military road. It was fierce with a lust for battle. You expected at any moment to hear a deep chord blown apart with a sudden explosion of heavy artillery.

Sgt. Reilly swore quietly and eloquently and then looked embarrassed. "Sorry, Father," he apologized. "Whenever I hear the singing of that Swastika Bund or come near anything else that they do…" He strode to the sacristy's little window and threw it open. The volume of sound rose perceptibly. The voices came clearer now and the words were German. I recognized the song; it was a marching song of Hitler Youth and I had heard it and hated it the preceding summer when I had traveled as a tourist in Germany and watched the regimentation of a nation. A people that sang from their love of music changed to a race that sang from their hatred of the enemies, hatred built up to synthetic wrath.

To the south side of the little chapel stood a public hall that constantly saw, on successive nights, meetings of social clubs, amateur boxing matches, receptions for young Jewish brides, Greek birthday parties, Italian christening festivities and now this meeting of the Swastika Bund.

Reilly stood glaring up at the lighted windows. I tugged Karl's arm and said, in a voice that I meant should reach Reilly's ears, "Wouldn't they have loved to lay their hands on Russian jewels? Wouldn't they have grabbed that wealth for their anti-American treasury?" Reilly whirled around with more speed and quickness of response than I had dared to hope for. His eyes bored into me with a searching intensity. "Anton," he said quietly, "you may be smarter about that than even *you* know." He whirled back to the little sacristy window and put his hand on the catch, as if he were trying to remember whether it had been open or whether in an unthinking, thoughtless gesture he had unlocked it.

Fr. Tierney, the generous fool, spoke up. "You unlatched it," he said. "It was locked."

Sargent Reilly muttered a low thanks and I could imagine the chain of reasoning that was linked in his mind. Was Fr. Tierney a guiltless man who could afford to throw aside a clue pointing to a possible real murderer? Or was he a clever man, who knew that this statement would make him, however guilty he might be, seem innocent? For the window led directly toward the back stairs that lead up into the Bund hall and if it had been open it would have been an easy step from the sacristy into the open air, and thence to the hall. Those jewels would be, the Bund would think, better in their hands than in the hands of a Russian countess. Only, as the priest had foolishly stated, the window had been locked and….

"So they got your jewels, didn't they?" I think we must have all whirled with a single mechanical impulse and I think we were all equally astonished, for framed, almost silhouetted in the doorway was a woman. At first glance, I didn't recognize her, then a second look brought back struggling memories of the social service clinic down the street, the Hallstead Center; of this woman who ruled it and coursed the district like some lean hunting dog; of children running away when she appeared and polite Italians standing in the doorway, listening as she talked to them in a flow of eager passionate words that might have made the men among them reach for a stiletto had they more than half understood; for she would fling the acid of her speech on their religion, offering the Center as a substitute for the Church.

She stood now in the doorway, lean, slightly disheveled, her suit not quite fitting, her hair not quite neat, the faint suggestion that she might be not quite clean. Her eyes, I could not help thinking, seemed not quite normal. But Reilly seized on a fact that in a moment we would all surely have noticed.

"How did you happen to know anything about the jewels?" The woman faced him and drew her lips into a thin line, savage in her contempt for him, writhing in her hate for the priest. She disregarded his question.

"This church," she waved into the semi-darkness, "once belonged to my center. Do you think I should've let them sell it if I had known it was for the Mass and the idolatry?" She included the icons in a gesture that was dramatically crammed with hate. "Well I asked her for those jewels, I told her what good they would do; the children, they would save them from the streets, the superstitions they would sweep from human minds; the mothers crushed under the millstone of childbearing to whom they would give freedom; I asked her for even a part of them to pawn for the services of another nurse, to sell to buy a bed, a swing for the playground, a year's service from a doctor; but she gave them to the Church—the Church!" she wrapped the word with a blanket of venom that made it seem the most awful of nouns. She looked at the priest.

"And now they've stolen them, these jewels—If you didn't steal them yourself!" she looked at the Sargent through eyes narrowing to a glinting squint. "I'm glad. They might have served humanity. The God to whom they were given hadn't strength enough to protect them from the thieves who wanted them more than He did."

As suddenly as she had come she swung away from the door and out into the aisle of the church. The hard leather of her low shoes clicked savagely; staccato messages of hatred, revenge, gratified resentment. I half expected Sgt. Reilly to spring down the aisle after her, instead he simply leaned against the door jam and watched her as she went down the aisle.

"Who's that queen of the may?" He asked nobody in particular.

Again Fr. Mark spoke in answer. "Her full name, I think, is Maud Bulling Whitecliff. She runs and, I rather think, owns the Hallstead Center. She's a thorn in the side of the churches—all of them—but how she knew…"

Reilly lifted a finger to a plainclothes man who had been standing against the far wall of the church.

"Tail her." he said briefly. But even as he did and the man obediently stepped forward the woman popped back into the church and almost screamed at Reilly across the brief distance. "Of course you'll have me followed! How did I know about the jewels? Eh? Well keep your men busy with someone who's guilty. And if I had the jewels do you think I'd be fool enough to let you find them when I know what they could do for me and *my* work?"

Again she disappeared and Reilly held the detective in check with a flick of his finger. "Skip it," he said quietly. "When we want her we'll find her easily enough. *Miss* Whitecliff, I suppose?"

"She claims she was never married," said Fr. Tierney.

"Isn't some man lucky?" Mused Reilly, without the slightest trace of humor in his voice.

The police had finished their search of the church and a uniformed sergeant came back to report.

"Nothing we could make of it," he said briefly. "Too many finger prints to make any of them important."

"We'll check it all at the station," said Reilly. And the police, after posting guards, disappeared. Then Reilly turned toward Fr. Tierney and the two of us.

"Of course you are, in a way, material witnesses, and I must ask you all to hold yourselves ready…"

And through the street door of the little church came the sudden roar of voices, angry voices, voices suited for brawls and battlefields and the raiding of small Jewish shops.

Reilly walked out into the sanctuary and peered out. The clamour swelled and above it I could distinguish the voice of an Irish policeman repeating his orders that nobody, no, not a God blessed soul was going to get in without a written official order. Reilly lifted his hand commandingly. "Let 'em in, O'Flanagan!" he cried and the officer resentfully stepped aside.

For a moment I felt myself transported back to the Berlin I had seen and pitied last summer. For down the aisle of the church swung, in military fashion, a tall man wearing riding breaches and leather putts and a brown shirt, across which was fastened a snug sand brown belt. On his dark head was a quasi military cap, marked with the Swastika.

Reilly moved forward a step so he held the man at the altar rail. Back of him came two associates dressed in almost the same uniform. Young, grim looking fellows, for all the world cut in the same grooves that had served for the making of storm troopers.

I shook myself violently. No, this wasn't Berlin or Munich; it was Chicago in America in dirty old Blue Island Avenue.

But the man was speaking. "Are you the officer in charge of this case?"

Reilly answered with a monosyllable that was like a blow.

"I," said the man in uniform, as if his name should open doors in the sides of mountains and lay pathways to the stars, "am Franz Schwartz. These are my lieutenants."

I could feel rather than see Reilly's left eyebrow lift a trifle. "Lieutenants?" He picked up the word and held it as he would a beetle; between thumb and forefinger. "I know only lieutenants who wear the army or navy or police or fire uniforms. What sort of lieutenants are these? And what kind of a fancy dress rig is that you've got on?"

Schwartz put his polished right boot upon the altar rail. For a moment I thought Reilly was going to kick it down, instead he insultingly lifted his own right shoe to an identical position and the two men stood facing each other without any pretense of the common decencies.

"I think," said the Bund leader, "that you will come to know these uniforms very well as time goes on. That's not, however, the reason I am here; to instruct you in the ways of the Swastika Bund. There's been a murder and an important theft."

Reilly gave no answer, no hint that an answer was expected of him.

"We feel that it is the duty of all decent Americans who hate the slimy communists and the dirty Jews who finance them, to help in a case of this kind. Fr. Tierney, there, is a friend of mine."

I must admit that I was amazed. I had never dreamed that Fr. Mark had the slightest connection with these professional ruffians. Then, when I saw the startled look on his face, I knew that he too was amazed so I waited for an explanation.

Reilly, without removing his foot or dropping his insulting attitude, turned toward the priest. "Is this," he said, indicating the Bund leader with deliberately crude jerk of his thumb, "a friend of yours?"

Fr. Tierney shook a positive head. "I have seen him on the street sometimes when he was going to his meetings but I've never spoken to him in my life."

Reilly swung insolently back to meet the Bund leader eye to eye. "Fr. Tierney is too much of a gentleman to say what I'll state plainly; that you are clearly a liar."

Schwartz shook that off with a twist of his shoulders. "Any man who hates the filthy Bolshevists as he does, who is preparing to go back to Russia—as I know he is—and undermine their power is a friend of mine and of my men of the Bund."

Reilly laughed shortly. "I am afraid, Fr. Tierney, that you are more picked upon than picking. Fortunately, one can always decline an offer of friendship."

Before Fr. Tierney could answer, Schwartz lifted his hand in a gesture that surprisingly commanded obedience. "Fr. Tierney may not know it, but he has for the past two weeks been getting envelopes from me and my Bund associates. We naturally signed our names as private individuals, not as Bund members. But I am proud now, Father, to be able to admit to our small contributions to your cause and your church."

From the flush that again rose to Fr. Tierney's face I knew that he must have been getting the envelopes and the money. They had seemed so innocent, now they proved so terrible a handicap.

Reilly kept shifting his gaze between the two men and he too clearly realized that the priest had been tricked into accepting the Bund's money.

But Schwartz was talking again in that deep, rumbling, authoritive voice of his. "Sargeant, I place my men at your disposal to help you solve this crime."

Reilly looked his blank refusal. "I rather fancy, Schwartz, that the recognized and official police force of the city can attend to matters of this kind, without help from fake soldiers, cheap imitations of European bullies." Schwartz smiled grimly. "Nevertheless, my men will be on the watch."

He took his foot from the altar rail and swung in military fashion toward the priest. "Sir, if you had stolen the jewels yourself, I should not have blamed you. Any means you took to help beat back these slimy communists I should consider honorable and noble. So, if you took Russian jewels to win back Russian people to decency and justice…"

Reilly's voice cut like a swung scimitar across the sentence. "I suppose, Schwartz, that you're not too dull to know what you are saying."

"Perfectly."

"And if you think it right for this priest to murder and steal for his cause maybe you think it would be right for your Bunders to murder and steal for *your* cause."

Schwartz met his inquisition without flinching. "Frankly, murder and theft are mere words when applied to the enemies of our cause or the goods of those who corrupt the world with their filthy teaching and practice. Does that answer your question?"

Reilly nodded slowly. "More than adequately." He placed his hand in an unexpected grip on the Bund leader's shoulder. Somehow with a hardly perceptible shrug, Schwartz tossed off the sergeant's hand.

"I dislike drama," he said.

"—in others," the detective added.

Schwartz looked over the head of the detective and straight at the priest. "Again, I say, Fr. Tierney: we of the Bund are your friends." He gutturaled a deep command. The lieutenants clicked their heels, stepped smartly aside, and he strode down the aisle of the church with the two men swinging in military precision behind him.

"Well," said Reilly quietly and then he grinned when the Irish patrolman at the door took a symbolic kick at the retreating forms of the Bunders. But Reilly's face grew instantly serious. "Father, you're not too lucky in your friends."

It was Karl who used his sentence as a cue line. "Well, if having us for friends is lucky," he said in a voice that he kept deliberately emotionless, "then you're in the luck. I know that Sgt. Reilly would laugh at the idea of your having anything to do with the whole miserable business. As for Pierre here and myself, well, being musicians of a sort, we practically have all the time in the world. I've always wanted to be an amateur detective."

"Well, what's a Sherlock without his Dr. Watson?" I demanded.

Reilly looked very official, so official that we all knew his posturing. "Very irregular. We professional 'tecs object to amateur meddlers." He grinned again. "I have a great gift, though, for looking the other way, so…" Serious again. "But, Fr. Tierney, I shall have to ask your word of honor that you will stay where I can reach you."

And as we stood together, a little huddle in the center of the dim sanctuary, I knew that a pact had been formed. The chase was on. But where was a clear scent, and where would it lead?

Chapter Three

The Church and the State combined to close that little church tighter than a waterlogged bureau drawer. When I came around the next morning to call on Fr. Tierney, virtually a prisoner in his little rectory, I found police at every locked door holding back the curious that had already gathered there, drawn by the smell of blood. And the Church had entered in too. It seems that the Catholic Church regards as desecrated a church in which any major crime has been committed. So even though this funny little Protestant church turned Greek Uniate had never been blessed or used for Catholic services, the Chancery Office had clamped another lock on the door in the form of a sign forbidding all services until further notice.

Well, the papers had taken the crime in hand and the radio announcers were holding high holiday. Although the papers hadn't come right out and made accusations on account of Catholic subscribers, they did some strong stressing of the priest's biretta and the fact that he had the only key to the sacristy that could be found.

"The papers," said a familiar voice at my shoulder, "have their old scandal scavenger tactics." It was Karl. He was brandishing a paper in his hand. I caught his elbow and steered him down the cosmopolitan thoroughfare, that is, Blue Island Avenue. He gave me his paper and as it was an edition that I hadn't seen, I read the section he pointed out. Clearly the writer thought Fr. Tierney was the man to play up as the suspect. In defying Catholic opinion he had done his best.

"Rotten stuff," I agreed. But I added in all honesty, "After all, the data thus far is rotten too. The biretta, the key, his motives—"

"What motives?" demanded Karl, his face darkly angry.

"Don't get hot like that," I answered. "I'm trying to see this as the police, the public, see it. He's crazy to get to Russia to work to convert the Bolshevists. The one thing in his way is the lack of money."

Karl flared. "You talk as if you thought he did it."

I grinned. "Don't be so stupid. I'm merely trying to be realistic.

We can't handle this case by playing ostridge or wishing for Santa Claus." We had swung around the block by this time and were once more in front of the rectory.

"You're right," Karl admitted grudgingly. "Let's go in and see him." As he rang the rectory bell, a policeman strode by and looked us over. Clearly Fr. Tierney was under close watch. Fr. Tierney was not alone. When he opened the door and silently shook hands with us we saw a woman in the room. She was slender and dark and beautiful; exotic as an orchid against Russian sables, artificial as a glass rose…and dramatic. She was pacing the little rectory which was not built for pacing.

The Countess Stefanska, it was she, accepted introductions with a fractional bow and, turning to Fr. Tierney, continued a gusher of speech that our entrance had evidently interrupted. The poor young priest! I felt sorry for anyone who had to face this Russian aristocrat hurdling English words over Russian ones in a rage of hysterical emotion. I shan't try to describe or transcribe her tirade. Briefly, it was clear that she still was waiting after all these years, since the death of the Tsar, to return to her parents' estates; to servants and lands. And the key to all this was to be had in the jewels.

I was sorry for poor Fr. Tierney, under the flow of her splattering anger. I was disgusted with her arrogance, her stagey aristocracy, her glaring conceit. But it was Sgt. Reilly who cut in and pulled her to a sudden stop. None of us had noticed his entrance. Evidently he had used a pass key. When he spoke, it was almost from the shadow of the street-door.

"Countess Olga," he said, "I realize that your jewels are very important and precious to you." Then his voice dripped chilled water. "But you must not forget that the man who was guarding them was killed. You should be a little distressed about that."

Her lip curled involuntarily but she was smart enough to snap out of it immediately. You could hardly have guessed that this was the spit-fire of a moment before. "I am sorry for poor Radolf," she said quietly. She had placed the situation in Reilly's competent hands. He gripped it firmly.

"Countess, I am sure of that."

Her dark eyes glowed gratitude for his understanding.

"However," he continued, "as no one seems to know the dead man, would you—"

She thrust the unspoken request away with a look of horror. Reilly was persuasive. "This man is, as you say, one of your people. Perhaps you once met in one of your haunts."

"If he was a servant," she replied haughtily, "I could not be expected to remember him and I do not frequent haunts."

But the sergeant crossed the room, took her by the arm, and piloted her toward the door and the street. His nod bade Fr. Tierney, Karl and myself to follow. We did. Reilly helped the Countess efficiently into the police car, motioned Fr. Tierney to get in, and, before he himself entered the car, told us to follow in a taxi.

As our taxi slipped into the wake of the police car I realized that we were headed toward the morgue. Being an artist, I dislike morgues intensely, as I dislike dead people. I followed them in, however, and stood back against the wall watching the Countess as Reilly led her to the draped figure on the cold marble table. She had drawn back in protest when she entered the cold room.

"Is it not enough that I lose my jewels? Must I look at dead men?"

"You are our only hope," said Reilly and he reached for the awful white covering that outlined the hidden figure. "If you can identify him…"

I know that we all stood on mental tiptoe. After all, he too was a Russian, even if only a humble sacristan. Perhaps Reilly thought Radolf was not so humble. The sacristan might have had his eyes on the jewels too; he might have known the Countess, heard of the jewels… I could almost feel her stiffening in the presence of death. Her repugnance, when Reilly drew back the white covering, was unmistakable. But it was an objective repugnance, a protest against looking on a dead person.

Suddenly we heard her scream. It was not a loud, dramatic scream this time, but one far back in her throat. Her face had gone chalk white under her rouge; her mouth was open in an ugly contrasting splash of lipstick. There was no doubt in my mind about the genuineness of her emotion.

"Ivan!" she cried, and she threw herself across the body of the dead man. We were all stunned, but Reilly was in command. He took the Countess's arms and gently lifted her up. There was in his look sympathy, but curiosity too. She broke away from him and this time signed herself with the Greek sign of the Cross and flung herself on her knees, praying in an agony of sincere grief. We waited, shaken by her sobs as if we were close enough to feel the physical violence of them.

At length she rose and turned to Reilly. "You must give me the body, of course," she said. She turned back to the dead sacristan and clung with her gloved hand to his senseless arm. "I've not seen him for years, since we were little children. It is he, undoubtedly, it is he."

Again we waited. Wild with curiosity that we were, we did not dare intrude our questions or hurry her broken comments. At length she gave the hoped-for explanation. "He must be buried as befits my brother, Prince Ivan."

Her brother! Had the sacristan known that these jewels were his sister's? And if he had known, wasn't it possible that he had regarded these jewels as his? Had he been defending them as the police thought? Or had he been planning to take them? Was it possible that, despite her authentic-appearing drama, the Countess and her brother were co-workers a double cross, a twisted conspiracy?

Motioning us to follow him, Reilly led the Countess to a little office. The explanation that under general pressure she gave through tears was all very queer—very unconvincing. Yet it was very Russian and sounded to me very probable because it made so little sense. I for one believed it.

The Countess and her brother, infants at the time, had escaped with their guardians. The guardians had kept the jewels for the day when the children could use them. Then the guardians died. The children passed from the care of White Russian to White Russian. The Countess and her brother were separated and finally out of touch with one another. The Countess became custodian of the jewels which the White Russians regarded as sacred, too important even to be pawned or sold. The brother and sister never met again. Did Ivan know anything about the jewels? She didn't know.

Had she meant to share them with him? She drew herself up indignantly. They were his as well as hers, she reminded us. Reilly pressed her no further.

Back we climbed into our cars and headed for the little rectory. The crowd around the church had increased; a mob standing silently gazing at the scene where blood had been shed—the powerful smell of blood had lured them, was holding them. The police car and our taxi pulled alongside the curb simultaneously. We got out hurriedly as the crowd, alert to any least move around the scene of the crime, surged forward curiously.

With difficulty the sergeant cleared a place around his car and into that space there darted the woman who, of all women living, was least like the Russian aristocrat that had just stepped onto the pavement. It was Maud Bulling Whitecliff, still dotty, divictionous; still acid.

"I'm glad they're gone," she cried, repeating her haunting vengefulness of last night. "Terribly glad."

The Countess looked at her in bewilderment, but before Reilly could swing his charge past the social service leader, Miss Whitecliff had gripped the Countess's arm tightly. "How little jewels mean to you! Something to wear to an opera, something to stick in altar vessels. That peasants starved around you in Russia; that the street teems with people hungry for the crusts you throw away; what does that matter to you? You give them to that thing." She swept her hand toward the church. "Almost I think that your God has punished you. You no longer have your jewels. The Church hasn't them. Where are they? The poor, my poor, may get them yet."

Reilly's voice was very low, but it reached the ears of those of us who stood in that amazing little circle. "Might I suggest, Miss Whitecliffe, that what you say almost makes me interested in you yourself. Is it possible that you know how those jewels will someday get to the poor?"

Miss Whitecliffe looked at him, sudden terror in her eyes. "No! No!" she gasped. "I know nothing about them, nothing!" And with quite unexpected strength she pushed through the crowd and fled down the street.

Reporters crowded around Reilly and a bulb snapped in the face of the Countess. Karl and I cut away. There was nothing more for us to learn there, or so we thought. We headed for a little restaurant and over coffee and rolls thrashed out the case. Karl, with that methodical mind of his, dissected the problem and laid all the elements on the table. I could almost see them on cards, indexed, marked in red or blue ink with the degree of suspicion measured to the least fraction of an inch. "Obviously," he summarized, "Fr. Tierney is not guilty."

But the noon editions of the papers had not been reassuring there. For want of anything better, the press still played up the fact that the priest's biretta was under the body; that he had the only key to the sacristy door, through which the murderer must have escaped, since Karl's entrance through the front door blocked that exit.

"Let us work with a strong motive for the robbery. There's Radolf himself," Karl went on, "and the Countess."

I shrugged my shoulders. "Russian aristocrats are rather careless of human life. But why should she want to steal her own jewels? There's Miss Whitecliffe. She knew of the jewels, had reasons for wanting them and is fanatic enough to do anything for her cause. And of course Franz Schwartz and his gang of Nazi cut-throats."

Karl's face was a study and surprise. "Knock me flat!" he said in a hushed voice. "I never thought of them."

"Why not?" I demanded. "Do you think that they'd hesitate at a little thing like knocking off a Russian or two to get their jewels to finance their cause? Do you think they'd run even the slightest risk of letting those jewels get back to the Soviet?"

"Let's follow that down," said Karl, banging the table. And then he suddenly became silent. "There's one other suspect, Pierre," he finally said quietly. This time I was puzzled. "Myself," he said at last.

I laughed out loud.

"You're kind to laugh," he said, " but after all, I was the one who found the body. I might have killed the man before I called you."

"Alright. Where did you hide the jewels? And how did you get time to hide them while I was coming into the church?"

"That does rather stump me," he said. "Just the same…"

I slapped the money for our sketchy lunch onto the table and laughed again. "Let's go out and trail Nazis," I said. Then I added in all sincerity, "Wouldn't I just like to nail this thing on them!"

But we unearthed nothing during the next three days and neither did the police, except—and it seemed to have no value unless to remove one of the suspicious clues that pointed to Fr. Tierney—the sacristy key. The police found it in an ash pit in an ally way back of the church. It had been tossed there by the criminal, or so the police figured. The criminal had evidently closed the sacristy door on his crime, turned the lock, carefully wiped the key and flung it into the ash pit whose contents would be emptied into an ash cart within a few hours. Only the ash cart had not arrived and the police had located the key, for whatever good it was.

Once a gambler, always a gambler, I guess, and I confess without shame that I stake a little bit on the horses. That is why the Barrier Smoke Shop knows me better than does the Union League Club. My regular bet is only two dollars but it's amazing what a lot of fun a born gambler can buy with a two dollar bet. Anyhow, the shop is an interesting place. Mel Clineman owns it, and Mel is an honest Jew and a nice one—a little radical in his viewpoints, but very conservative about horses. His partner is Sean O'Rafity who talks with a Dublin brogue and votes a straight Communistic ticket. The third member of the shop is a little fellow called, in strange Polyglot, Jock Lyndski. Nobody seems to know much about him. The people that hang around bookies don't pry very much into antecedents.

On the fourth futile day after the murder I dropped into the Barrier which crouches in the shadows where Blue Island Ave flows into Halstead Street. Mel Clineman waved at me as I entered. Sean O'Rafity came and stood at my elbow as I studied the entries for the fifth at Latonia.

Down the long counter Lyndski was taking a bet from a Jap I'd seen there before and who had always bet more heavily than the cut of his clothes seemed to warrant. I shrugged my shoulders in the direction of the Jap.

"Who's the Oriental?" I asked Sean. But Sean, who knows everything about horses and whose only interest outside of horses is communism, had a communist's personal distain of individuals. All he did was grunt. So I picked Playboy in the fifth, laid my little bet and meandered off. I was sorry later that my interest in the murder hadn't kept me too busy for bets, for Playboy finished somewhere in the lead of the sixth race; and as a strange thing called coincidence would have it, the Barrier burst into the murder case the very next day. Sgt. Art Reilly was sitting with Karl and Fr. Tierney when I entered the little rectory. Reilly held up a single unset stone. Nobody needed to explain that.

"One of the missing jewels?" I asked, taking the stone, though the question was much more of a statement. It was a perfect white diamond, two or three karats in weight. I gave it back to Reilly and sat down and waited for him to speak.

"Do you know the Barrier Smoke Shop?" Reilly asked.

"If for a minute you are a friend and not an arm of the law," I confessed, "I will admit that I sometimes lay down a little bet there."

Reilly grinned. "As your friend, I'll say nothing about it to the arm of the law. Well anyhow, you're not the only one that puts down bets there. It seems there is a Jap—"

"I've seen him," said I. "He's a regular there."

"Set a regular to catch a regular," was Karl's unkind comment.

Reilly waited until the laugh at my expense had subsided, and resumed. "A little fellow named Jock Lyndski, a clerk in the Barrier, turned this in at a pawn shop we've been watching. We picked him up of course, and he told us that it was left at the Barrier to cover some losses incurred by this little Jap."

"What's the Jap's name and where does he live?"

Reilly shook his head. "We don't know yet, but my men are on his trail. We'll find out, and if there is one jewel there, probably there are more, and if there are more…"

I looked a little incredulous. "Will you please tell me how you're so sure that this single unset stone is one of those that were stolen?"

Reilly laughed. "We're not sure, that is, not quite sure. With a stone like that, that facet not modern in style, but cut according to the fashion of a hundred years or more ago…"

Karl and I wandered out into the early evening. If this Jap had possession of the stones, how did he get them? Was he working for himself or for someone else? Karl and I puzzled about this with a sense of growing exasperation.

"I always knew," said Karl, "that jewels drew the strangest birds of prey in the world, but that they should draw a sort of world wide international congress…"

And as he spoke I saw striding toward us down the street Franz Schwartz. He was not in his Bund uniform but you could feel the uniform in every stride he took, every beat of his leather heels on the pavement. If he had suddenly snapped his hand into a "Heil Hitler" salute and started to goose-step I should not have been even mildly surprised.

"Let's dodge him," said Karl.

"Dodge that big bully? Not I." I preferred to face the fellow and see how the progress of the case during the past days had effected him.

Almost before we had finished our brief dialogue, Schwartz was upon us, grinning a grin that displayed every tooth for exhibition. I knew just how Little Red Riding Hood must have felt when she commented on her supposed grandmama's bridge work.

"Good evening," Schwartz said cheerfully. Even under his carefully articulated English I caught the guttural that was not of our shores. We each tossed him our greetings in F sharp and B minor respectively, but he caught us by the arms and hurried us toward a dimly lighted cavern. "I owe you boys a drink," he said, and waved off any protest that might have been quivering on Karl's tongue.

Three large foamy beers were placed before us and Schwartz lifted his stein in a toast. "To America," he said. "May she find true peace and safety from her enemies."

"If you're thinking what I'm thinking," said Karl, "you probably will choke on that toast."

Schwartz laughed as if that were a great joke and started to talk baseball, the murder, his deep respect and affection for Fr. Tierney, the latest movies, then suddenly—"Reinhardt," he said, "with a German name like yours, and by the way, isn't Anton a German name too?"

"Don't forget the 'Pierre'," I shot back. "Nothing German about that."

"But Karl," he continued, "Karl Reinhardt." He positively rolled the names around his tongue affectionately. "That's a magnificent German name for you, though I think you've dropped a few consonants between the fatherland and here."

Karl glared into his stein and said nothing.

"One thing Hitler has taught us," said Schwartz, wiping the foam from his lips, "is this; Once a German always a German. There is all over the world a German people bound together by common ties of blood, culture, race, loyalties. Karl, you are still one of us."

I could feel Karl bristle. I nudged him under the table. *Let the man talk,* I thought. *He'll hang himself or give us a chance to hang him.*

"We need young men like you in the Bund, my friend. As a rule, men come asking me to admit them. I don't ask them, but when I meet a young fellow like you with all the qualities that make a great German, a chap who in the old country would be one of Hitler own bodyguards; Karl, will you join us in the Bund?"

Even my second nudge, far from gentle this time, could not keep Karl in his place. He was on his feet and, from the tenseness of his fists, I expected him at any moment to hurl the stein which was still filled with beer into the Bund leader's face. Instead he hurled words, and they were strong, monosyllabic words all of them summed up to the general effect that he'd see Schwartz in a spa, moreover, even a Nazi concentration camp before he'd join the Bund. Schwartz took to his heels.

"The dog!" growled Karl. "The dirty dog! To ask me to join his stinking Bund! Me, American right through to the core of my heart. Me, with ancestors in the Civil War and the Revolution."

I let his boil come to a milder simmer and then I said, as quietly as I could, "Karl, for once I think you've made a mistake. Not that I don't agree that his invitation is a rank insult, but suppose that what we think possible is true. Suppose that the Bund did know of the jewels, wanted them for their cause, robbed the safe, killed Radolf; who'd ever find out all this except a member of their organization? And if that member happens to be you, well, we'd clear Fr. Tierney immediately and pin this crime on the culprit."

It took me two hours of talking and a succession of beers to get him to the point where he was listening. Finally it dawned on him that this really was a great idea. We left the tavern and walked the streets until we met Schwartz again. Then, still glowing with our idea, we offered to join the Bund. Only when the calm light of morning came shining in through our window did we wonder whether we made fools of ourselves. And then it was too late to pull back from our membership and what we honestly regarded as a troop of our country's most relentless foes.

Chapter Four

The papers, of course, did their usual hounding of police during the next week of apparent inaction. The little Greek Uniate church of St. Sergus remained, under the double seals of the Church and State, closed tighter than a Scotchman's safe-deposit vault. I dropped around regularly, with or without Karl, and though no arrest had been made and no slightest clue found to the missing jewels, I knew that Fr. Tierney was feeling intensely the suspicion under which he must inevitably be. He talked things over with his bishop who was sympathetic and understanding but who wished that, until the seven day wonder of the murder and theft had blown over, the little church remain tightly sealed and all talk of the work that the young priest meant to do in Chicago and later on in Russia be kept far in the background.

Anyhow, when Karl and I agreed to join Schwartz and his Bund we let ourselves in for more than we had suspected. Schwartz's first reaction had been hardy, almost boisterous pleasure. When, later that evening we had announced our change of mind and heart and our determination to join in with him and his fellow Hitler-ites, he pounded our backs lustily, insisted on plying us with more beer, assured us of his delight at our having seen the justice of the Nazi cause and the glory of Pan-Germanism under the mighty Führer and even gave us a preliminary informal introduction to the Bund members. And then came a change of front.

We were visited by a series of men, all trying desperately to look like storm troopers, that needed only one quick jump to be in full uniform, who pried into our personal lives, asked us searching questions about our Arian ancestry and left behind them small books—some in German, some in English—that were, we learned, our textbooks. There's no Jewish in either Karl or myself but I found out that once, when a big lug demanded to know how far back we could trace the purity of our blood Karl and I had had a common impulse. I had wanted to say, "I can trace it to yesterday afternoon when we drank beer with Schwartz." And Karl had had it on the tip of his tongue to say, "Well, I had a maternal uncle whose name was Israel Cohan but I think he was an Irishman."

We took Sgt. Reilly into our confidence and though he decided that officially, he had better do nothing about it, he shook hands with us approvingly and said, with a glint in his Celtic eyes, "I wonder whether I couldn't get in too. *Reilly* is a fine old German name."

Well, we studied our textbooks together and writhed at the false history that made attacks on democracy, we listened to uniformed storm troopers instruct us in the ritual of initiation. We were glad to find that in any case we'd not be required to take an oath until at least two or three months later.

"My conscience was bothering me," Karl confessed. "How could I take an oath to follow these scoundrels when all the time I mean--"

"Skip it!" I cried, "Don't get me jittery too. As candidates we take no oath."

"I wish I could talk it over with Fr. Tierney," he said, but I waved my arms wildly at the idea. The poor priest had troubles enough of his own without our piling our consciences on top of his. The night before the Bund meeting, Reilly, Karl, Fr. Tierney and I met in the priest's parlour to bring all developments up to date. The Barrier Smoke Shop had been watched but the Jap that left the antique cut diamond had not reappeared. Maybe it wasn't part of the missing jewels anyhow, we agreed. The Countess Olga had buried her slain brother. There was a simple ceremony, over which Fr. Tierney had presided, in a small convent chapel out of the normal range of reporters. She had settled herself down in the Morris Hotel where she could be reached, Reilly assured us, at any time.

"Though she may know a lot more than she told us, I don't believe she would have killed her own brother to get the jewels," Reilly pointed out. We admitted that that did sound more twisted than a permanent wave, and we parted feeling that we were fighting our way through cobwebs that could hardly be seen yet kept lining us with their persistent clinging; webs fragile and intangible and yet holding us like ropes woven to moor in an Atlantic liner. If the papers were giving the red jewels of white Russia a wonderful ride, they were not ignoring the sharp upward rise of the Bund in the city. And when Schwartz announced on the appointed day that in a big Westside auditorium (scene of prize fights and charity balls, and national presidential nominations) he was rallying around him the noblest exiled sons and daughters of New Germany, the papers got right on the job and played up the meeting in screaming headlines. And Schwartz, who loved the camera with the love of a Hollywood Hopeful, gave them plenty of shots of himself, looking like a blend of Mussolini and Hitler, and fed them a tall line about saving America from the "Stinking Reds", who, he said, were hiding under the patronage of the government.

The last detachment of storm troopers that arrived brought us our uniforms, and we tried them on with all the enthusiasm of victims being fitted with handcuffs or straight jackets or a complete coat of mustard plasters. And when we looked at each other, brown shirted, visor capped, with a Swastika pinned on our arms, and a sand brown belt adorning our noble chests, we first gritted our teeth in a rage and then saved the situation by sitting down and roaring with laughter.

"If," said Karl at last, in a strangled half whisper, "we go through all this monkey business and then find out nothing…"

"Don't worry," I reassured him, "we'll pin this on Schwartz and his gang, or my name isn't Anton."

The newspapers played up that particular Bund meeting with such a spread that there is no need for my telling the story in detail. It took all our courage to get into those fool uniforms, slip disguising raincoats over us and plow our way through the crowd that milled outside the big palladium. We fought through a twisting cue of Jewish pickets all carrying placards denouncing the arrival of Hitlerism in the States. We saw throughout the crowd legionnaires, their jaunty service caps tilted at pugnacious angles, and their fists just aching to start a haymaker right up from the pavement. Sound trucks were getting the noises and the shouts on discs for news reels and the news photographers were shooting bulbs in such rapid succession that if the bulbs had made a noise you'd have thought the place was being bombed.

We had been given careful instructions; we gained the side entrance, were marshaled into the dressing room, relieved of our coats, searched most painstakingly by guards in full Bund uniforms and with our fellow candidates formed into a full line of march. I know I looked around me, wondering how these other chaps had got themselves into the mess. For the most part they were normal young fellows like those you see hanging around a pool room or leaning against the corner drug store, though among them were others whose accents were so thick a rabbit could have run along them without sinking in. Karl and I found ourselves between a young mechanic that, according to his story, had been out of work for two years and a filing clerk that was bored of his job and hated the Jew that bossed him. We got their stories while we waited for orders. The mechanic believed that Hitler had given every young man in Germany a job, "and that's more than Roosevelt's done," he said. The young filing clerk hated the dull, pointless work at which he spent his day and, "I'd like to get that Jew whose earning five times as much as I am just because he's got no scruples and will put through any kind of dirty deal."

Our drill sergeant snapped his orders and we stood at attention. Up in front of us appeared an American flag, flanked by two other flags marked with giant Swastikas. A drum corps began to ruffle, bugles blared forth, the doors of our dressing rooms swung open and out we marched into the hall.

It hurt so—the whole shameful performance—that I could've cried. Karl's jaws were working savagely, but I'll bet the others thought it was just the grim determination of a born Nazi bent on bringing these United States to toe the line. The papers played it all up; the hall, the meeting, those American flags crossed with Swastikas, the big pictures of Washington, Lincoln, Hitler, Goering and Goebbels at the end of the hall, the play of the search lights that swept around the audience like intangible finders, the mass battalion of storm troopers, a solid, brown, stern, unsmiling block in the center of the hall.

So it's all old stuff to most of you, but it wasn't old stuff to us who marched stiffly down the aisle toward the seats that were kept for us in the front of the auditorium. Maybe you don't think that we had our emotions all milling around inside of us like things that were being flipped in a giant cocktail mixer. Maybe you'll be surprised to know that for a moment the mass of people, the rhythm of the drums and the impelling screech of the bugles, the sound of our own marching feet and the massing of flags all around us, really got into my blood.

I was part of something big, terrible, forbidding, prophetic of power. I had to shake myself into remembering the truth; this was not a proud march into glorious standards, an assembling of men dedicated to noble purposes. This was a demonstration that was meant to shake the liberties of my country and plunge me under the power of tyranny.

We filed into our places while around us roared the applause and the undercurrent of boos and groans that blended with the shouts and handclappings. At a signal, the light sharply dimmed, a single floodlight flung a silvery white circle into the center and into it snapped Franz Schwartz and the two men that regarded themselves as his Goebbels and Goering.

We all snapped to attention and at a ringing blast of the trumpet shot our hands forward in the "Heil Hitler" salute. Out and back and out and back and out again to hold them there while those who knew the song picked up and shouted "the hoarse whistle." Another blast of the trumpet and we sat down. Then Schwartz talked and as he talked I knew that the man had power, the gripping power of eloquence that rises superior to any question of what is said, and becomes a matter merely of the white heat that burns in the heart and the throat of the speaker and fuses his words into steal armour and ringing swords and tanks and artillery, massed to take over the world.

We listened, Karl and I, but you read the speech in the papers: the laudation of Germany, the cursing of England, a fiery attack upon Communists, a masterly indictment of all enemies of democracy…except those that had rallied under the twisted cross.

Only when Schwartz came to his conclusion did Karl and I grow tense in anticipation.

"Whatever comes from Russia," he thundered, "is cursed, make no mistake. There is a blight upon that awful monster who once was a bear that walked like a man and who is now a giant that has the soul of a gorilla, the morals of a jungle tiger and the crawling secrecy of a snake in the hot grasses of India. Whatever comes to us from Russia brings death and destruction with it even, yes, even jewels that are placed under the care of the Church. Not even the touch of the Church can take away the curse of anything Russian. You know what I mean; an innocent priest that we love and respect lies under the suspicion of crime. What is his real crime? That, like us, he meant to fight the Communistic giant. Yes, to track that monster even into the heart of red Russia and slay it with the gentle blows of the crucifix. They hate him as they hate us, my friends, my brothers of another cross. I shall return to that priest, another victim of the Russian curse, in a moment. We stand for true government, not the lumbering, clumsy, stumbles of false democracy. Not the observed pretense that an Arian warrior is no better than a Jewish pawnbroker; the true government of discipline and obedience, courageous, glorious leadership and massing of men of pure blood, men that love high culture and dream of a world in which a superior race shall set the standards for lesser breeds. For this we need money. My friends," his voice dropped as if what he meant to say was so confidential that he intended it only for a few ears. "Never fear; we shall find that money. I might almost say to you, we *have* found the money."

I felt Karl's knee hit mine in sharp hint. So Schwartz was openly bragging that he had found money. Where? This was a crowd of relatively poor men, laborers, artisans, clerks without resources. Schwartz's bragging could mean only one thing, and involuntarily my hand closed over Karl's knee. Schwartz had the missing jewels! Wasn't it clear? We needn't have joined this fool organization to learn the truth. Schwartz had just admitted it openly from the platform! All this was telegraphed between us in the impact of Karl's knee against mine and my answering hand replying wordlessly that I understood, and that the trail was hot.

But Schwartz was going ahead with his speech. "But this poor priest!" he cried. "This man who has been unjustly touched with the blight of all things Russian. We must stand by him. His enemies are our enemies and we are his friends. If the stupid democratic laws of this country lay their hand upon him we shall be ready to rise to his defense. Ready with men and money. Comrades!" he called, and a half hundred uniformed Bundsters holding boxes in their hands leaped forward. "Go among our friends an collect the money that we will need to hire the finest defense lawyers in the country, if Fr. Tierney should fall into the hands of the stupid police of this city."

I caught Karl just in time. He was almost on his feet, white, furious, trembling with wrath but I pulled him down. "Quiet, you fool!" I hissed above the clamour.

"But don't you see what this does to Fr. Tierney?" he almost wept.

Of course I did. It branded him as the friend of the Bundsters. It marked him as one receiving full support from them. The thought was publicly classed in with the Jew beaters, the Nazis, the anti-democrats, and if things went bad his case would be hurt, not by evidence, but by the poisoned kiss of these false friends.

All around was wild confusion. The collectors were pouring through the hall and the audience was wildly applauding and angrily booing as men leaned forward to contribute or to fight off the hands that reached out to pull the paste work containers from the grip of the storm troopers. And from the stage, Schwartz surveyed the chaos with that undisguised contempt he reserved for all assemblies of people, even those that came in answer to his call.

"Let's go!" I cried and grabbed Karl by the wrists. The two on either side of us looked up in surprise. As for the others, they saw in us merely two more storm troopers headed for some unknown mission and stood aside to let us pass or growled at us or applauded us as we shouldered through the mob.

How we found him, I don't know, except that we had a way of turning up at unexpected minutes. But as we flung out of the dressing room where we had gone to get our raincoats we ran flush into Sgt. Reilly. Karl almost cried out in relief.

"Nice meeting?" said Reilly sardonically.

"Did you hear the speech?" Karl demanded and I stood on mental tiptoe waiting for his answer.

"I did," said the detective.

"Practically," I prodded, "an admission that he has the jewels."

I was surprised that Reilly lifted doubting eyebrows. "No get," he answered.

"They're poor, haven't a red cent—not really. Now Schwartz from the platform brags that they have the money enough for their cause."

Reilly turned quickly and we fell in at his heels. From somewhere two other men joined us and we cut into the street through the increasingly riotous crowd to the back entrance where a quick display of badges gained us admition. It was the performance entrance to the palladium and Reilly bolted up the narrow staircase with the rest of us in hot pursuit. In front of a dressing room marked with a large star stood two storm troopers at attention. When we came in sight they laid their hands onto the clubs that were at their side. Reilly flashed a badge.

The taller trooper barked. "This is the dressing room of the leader, no one comes in here."

"Says you," answered Reilly and one of the trailing detectives pressed something hard against to taller trooper's back. As he did so the other trooper made a quick move and headed for the narrow stairs.

"Grab him!" yelled Reilly. I never had more real pleasure than I had when I threw my whole weight on this man and the other detective caught him from behind and swung him around toward the door. "Push them into the dressing room and get in too. If Schwartz hears we're here he won't come up."

We were all crowed into the small room; the two troopers standing with their faces to the wall. "You, men," and he signaled his detectives, "get into the uniforms and stand at the door. Quick! Because if he arrives and finds the men gone he'll run for it."

"Why should he?"

We all wheeled. The voice was so calm, so without tremour or emotion. In the doorway as unperturbed as if he were walking into his own breakfast nook was Franz Schwartz. He walked into the dressing room, closed the door behind him and stood tapping a cigarette against his thumb. Heavens, how that man loved dramatics! And what an actor he was. I admired him even as I wanted to reach for his chin.

Reilly's orders soon emptied the dressing room of everyone except Schwartz and Karl and myself.

"Cigarettes?" asked Schwartz, holding out his pack toward us in a gesture of steady insolence and affront.

Reilly waved it away for all of us and stood in front of the Bund leader, glaring and really angry. "So, from the stage tonight you practically admitted you have the Russian jewels," he barked.

"On the contrary, I said that anyone who came in contact with them was doomed." Schwartz was all ironic courtesy.

"You know how to remove that curse; by turning them to Bund purposes," retorted the detective.

Schwartz lit his cigarette slowly, seeming to hold the match deliberately before his face as if inviting us to see how utterly undisturbed he was, how quite without fear. And I must admit that he did the part convincingly. "Gentlemen," he cried at last. "We of the Bund have other sources of money besides clumsy stolen jewels. There are those abroad who think our work important enough to…shall we say, simply *encourage* it. And if I had stolen the jewels, or knew where they were, I may be a stupid fool as you gentlemen complementarily think me, but not quite fool enough to make statements that would set you on the trail of the jewels."

We knew he was entirely right. Karl had the look of someone caught in an intolerably stupid situation. Reilly flicked that left eyebrow thoughtfully and by so doing dismissed this lead.

Schwartz sank into a chair languidly and said, with some reason, "This has been a trying evening, gentlemen, and I am a little tired. If you have nothing further…"

"Come," said Reilly and we started toward the door. But Schwartz was by no means through.

"As for you," he said picking out Karl and myself, "I confess you fooled me. I thought you were men worthy of the shirt you now wear. I do not like spies and traitors; I do not like men who are prepared to take oaths falsely. We members of the Bund do not forgive trickery." He turned away from us. "I suppose that if any accident should befall you your friend Sargeant Reilly would come straight to me."

Reilly echoed him with emphasis. "*Straight to you, Schwartz.*"

"…With the same success, no doubt, that you had tonight. Don't let me keep you further, gentlemen. I am sure you still have a great many things unfinished. You seem to specialize in unfinished business."

We sat together over coffee and sandwiches though none of us, I confess, showed much sign of appetite.

"I still believe it's Schwartz and his crowd," I began.

Karl looked at me almost in disgust. "What a mess we got ourselves into! And Schwartz walked out without our laying a finger on him."

"Yet," I protested, "if he has the jewels, as I believe he has, wouldn't he take precisely the stand he did take?"

"Precisely," Reilly agreed and then rose. "I'll be back in a minute—just a phone call to headquarters."

We were a bedraggled and discouraged pair, sitting there at the table; our raincoats turned up to hide the disgraceful uniform we wore, our pride in our pockets and pretty battered. And Fr. Tierney more involved than ever in the awful mess. I don't think we exchanged a word; I know I let my coffee go cold. And Reilly came back to the table and sat down heavily as if he were carrying an unseen load; a new problem awaited secret.

We both looked up in interest. Anything could happen now and leave us unsurprised. He soon relieved us. "We've located another of the missing jewels."

"No!" we cried in perfect duet.

"The Jap appeared at the Barrier smoke shop late this evening and left another one."

"Not another unset stone?" I protested, for even the antique cut of that last stone left the matter doubtful as evidence.

"A ring this time," said the detective. "A small gold band with ancient carvings on the mounting. And in the center a beautiful flawless ruby. No doubt about it; it's one of the stones. Headquarters rushed it to the Countess who identified it at once and the Jap is waiting for us in jail."

We got out of the taxi, bolted up the stairs and followed the turnkey to the cells. In one of them a figure wrapped in a too-large overcoat was sleeping peacefully. It was, no doubt of it, the Jap from the Barrier Smoke Shop. He woke up and smiled blandly as if he had been waiting for us and was very glad to see us.

"Where," demanded Reilly, fixing him with a tough eye and an extended finger, "where did you get that ruby ring you offered to the bookmakers tonight?"

"From a lady," answered the Jap in perfect English, without the slightest trace of accent.

"A lady," retorted Reilly and irony just dripped in acid globules from his tongue, "—just likes your looks, I suppose, and said 'Here, darling, is a little keepsake'."

The Jap shook his head without altering a fraction of his smile. "No," he said. "The lady for whom I am butler asked me to take it."

"Oh," said Reilly still running strong on sarcasm, "so you're not a burglar; you're a butler. And I suppose you wouldn't want to tell us the name of the lady."

"Why not?" asked the Jap. "I am sure that smart officers like you"— and he included us all in the gesture—"would find out anyhow. I got the ring from a very fine lady. I'm sure you all know her; Mrs. Hilary Goodspeed."

That set us all back on our heels. I know Karl gasped out loud.

"Why!" cried Reilly in disgust. "What kind of yarn is this? She's the wife of a United States senator."

"Precisely," said the Jap. "Is there anything else you'd like to know?"

There was plenty, but when a prisoner is that ready and willing to hand it out, it sounds too phony to be good news. You don't go around pinning jewel thefts and murders on the wives of the United States senators. Or do you?

Chapter Five

The lean looking chap that was taking an uncommonly long time to light his pipe gave Sgt. Reilly the slightest flicker of recognition as we turned up the private driveway that led to Senator Goodspeed's beautiful home.

"Webber," said Reilly by way of explanation, "we've had a man on the house steadily since we picked up that ring and the Jap."

Reilly pressed the doorbell. Almost at once the door was opened and we got the start of our lives. For smiling at us from the doorway was our friend the Jap, now in impeccable livery, bowing a welcome.

"I was expecting you," said he.

"That's more than we can say about you," snapped Reilly, and he stood waiting for an explanation.

"Are you coming in?" asked the Jap by way of flat statement. "I am so glad that the States have that quaint custom of bale, and Mrs. Goodspeed's lawyer was generous."

So that was it; the Senator's wife had sprung the Jap through her lawyer.

We stepped into the pleasantly dim reception hall. Dexterously the Jap-butler took Karl's hat and mine, but we took them back when we saw that Reilly was holding onto his.

"Tell Mrs. Goodspeed that I want to see her, at once," Reilly was snapping again.

The Jap disappeared. We took seats in the little reception room off the hall and waited impatiently in an atmosphere that breathed cultured luxury and ease. Certainly nothing here suggested murder or theft. Nor was there such a suggestion in the gracious lady that swept into the room in a long trailing housecoat that could have been worn by a leading soprano when she walked to the footlights for a big solo. And for the next ten minutes we felt as if we, not she, were the ones under suspicion. I never saw another grown dame carry off the situation with such an air. She regretted that her butler was an incorrigible gambler, but he was. She forgave him that, though, in view of his devoted service and the way he had with

Helen's—that was her daughter—twins and her own three children. Naturally she knew nothing whatever of a place called the Barrier Smoke Shop and as for Russian jewels…Well, obviously!

It was magnificent. You'd have sworn she had no more to do with the thing than did the wife of President Roosevelt. In fact, Eleanor would be more likely to have been around at the time. Mrs. Goodspeed was either innocent as the most recent arrival in a maternity ward, or the best actress I'd ever seen, on or off stage.

No, she didn't know the Countess Olga. No, she had never heard of the Russian jewels. No, she did not know there was such a place as St. Sergius Greek Uniate Church. And she did not wish to detain us longer on what was obviously a waste of the gentlemen's time.

And we were out on the street, still holding our hats, and trying to get back our breath with the Jap butler smiling his hand carved smile as he closed the door slowly and with dignity behind us.

"If you ask me—" Reilly began.

"We certainly do," said Karl and I in chorus.

"The lady is superb, the book makers are also careful book keepers. Let's look up the lady's record at the Barrier.

Lyndski was alone when we came into the smoke shop. It was too early for the usual gathering of the fans, and only a stray customer or two were patiently studying the form sheets and reading the blackboards for the day's scratches and odds. I wondered where Moe and the Irishman were; neither was in sight.

Lyndski bowed professionally and asked us what we were picking today.

"We're picking up a little information, my fine federal friend," said Reilly, "which you'll be good enough to hand over or else…" and he flashed his badge.

I thought at the time that either gangsters were beginning to talk like detectives or detectives like gangsters. And evidently Lyndski was used to moving for both, for he was in the back room and out again with a thick ledger in no time at all. And Reilly, with the two of us craning over his shoulder, was working through those grisly pages with expert skill.

It was amazing to see the names, famous in city affairs, society and education that popped up at us from the pages of that book of gambling doom. Only no record of Mrs. Goodspeed. Oh, there was plenty for the Jap: Eturah Najoki_was his name, which sounded like the name of a Pullman car. And he was debited on those books for the amount of eleven thousand three hundred and seventy-six dollars. In spite of the fact that he had an apparent run of luck lately and wiped out another debt of nine thousand.

"I'm surprised," said Reilly, looking at Lyndski, who had been coming and going between the shop and the backroom. "Very much surprised at you'll carry an account like that up into the thousands. How do you know the Jap will make good?"

Lyndski said nothing but shrugged in a foreign sort of fashion and waved back at the book we were inspecting. That was of course the answer. During the past three years Najoki had been in and out of the red a dozen times. Once he had owed up to fifteen thousand and had wiped the account out with one big check. And if he had made up his losses in the past, wasn't it reasonable enough to expect that he would make them up in the future? Except that on the salary of a butler, even in the home of a United States senator and even with money of his own...

Reilly closed the book with a bang and we headed back for headquarters. The two of us planted ourselves in the pressroom while Reilly disappeared briefly. When he came back he had two small sheets of paper in his hand.

"Look," he said and pulled us out into the corridor. The two papers had only partial thumbprints, that is, one of them was partial; the other was practically complete. But even from the partial prints it was clear that the two papers indicated the same thumb.

"Whose?" I demanded.

"That," said Reilly, indicating the partial print, "was taken from the inside of the stolen ring. The other we got by a little ingenuity that we needn't waste time on now. And both are Mrs. Goodspeed's."

"Meaning?"

"That the lady had that ring in her hand, that she must have given it to the Jap, and that if he carried it to the Barrier he's just a front for her. Which explains, of course, how a Jap on a butler's salary is that far in debt, and calls for a lot of explaining from the good Mrs. Goodspeed."

This time the door of the senator's mansion was opened by a trim little maid. When we told her that we wanted to see Mrs. Goodspeed she took us down a long hallway, knocked on the heavy folding door and opened it for us to reveal a magnificent library and at a desk near the deep window the much publicized figure of the Senator from Illinois; and standing near him, her back to the light and a handkerchief twisted feverishly in her hands, was his wife. It needed no strong light to tell us she had been crying.

The senator rose. "Gentlemen," he said, "be seated." And we felt like end men in a minstrel show being signaled by an expert interlocutor. "My wife," he said, "has told me of your previous visit and she has also explained the unfortunate situation in which she finds herself." He took her hand and pressed it affectionately. Clearly there was still much love between them and the Senator had taken upon himself her predicament. She left the room and we were alone with senator.

"I don't know just how much you gentlemen know," he began, lighting a cigar after having passed the cigar box to us, "but…"

"We know plenty," said Reilly. "Your wife is some eleven thousand dollars in the red at the Barrier Smoke Shop. The account is in the name of your Jap butler but he's clearly a front. And her finger print was on the ring that he turned in as a pawn yesterday. The ring, as you probably also know, is part of the jewels that were stolen in that murder job in the sacristy of St. Sergius' church."

If we expected a tirade of denunciation and excuses we were amazed. The senator sat smoking quietly for a moment, then he looked up from his thoughtful study and faced us calmly. "Gentlemen," he said, "I shall not try to bluster my way out of this or to tell you some fabulous story."

I think we all felt completely deflated at this turn in the events. Was it possible that he meant to plead guilty for his wife? And how in thunder could she have been involved in it anyhow? That question was written large on the faces of both Reilly and Karl.

The senator resumed. "My wife, I regret to learn, has been placing bets that are far beyond her income. I shall—" he coughed and for a moment seemed acutely worried "—pay those debts immediately. May I trust you to see that this sordid bit of family history does not reach the press?" The senator was deeply concerned.

Reilly waived this aside as irrelevant. He felt that he was on the edge of an important revelation and details annoyed him. "But what about the ring and the other unset gem?" he demanded. "What's your wife got to do with them?"

The senator's embarrassment was obvious. "Gentlemen," he said, "you'll forgive me for what seems an incredible story. But this is a case where truth is stranger than fiction."

"I've noticed that," said Reilly, cynically incredulous.

The senator rose and paced up and down. Clearly he had no expectation that we would believe the story he meant to tell. Yet his worried air indicated that, strange as it was, he himself believed the story. "How can I ever convince you that this is true?" he began. But now the door through which Mrs. Goodspeed had just left the room opened again and she was back. Traces of tears were now gone; she had repaired her make-up and she moved towards us, all drama and persuasive beauty. I must confess that for her age the good lady had plenty of charm and much, much excellent drama.

"Darling," she said to the senator, "perhaps they'll believe me if I tell them the truth exactly as it is."

He sank into his big chair and she stood leaning slightly against the desk. Her hands white from the grip she kept on the top and, one felt, on her courage. "You know how deeply I am in debt," she went on in a rush of words. "Gambling is a vice that grows and grows. It swept me down at last. But this is what I myself do not understand. Some mornings ago, as I sat at my dressing table, I noticed a small package among my perfumes. It was a plain box; stamped, addressed in square handwriting. I opened it and out fell, into my palm, that strangely cut diamond and the ring that you found yesterday."

I could positively hear Reilly snort, though he tried to hide his distain of this flimsy story.

"I know it sounds ridiculous," burst in the senator, but his wife lifted her white hand, silencing him gently.

"You must believe me!" she cried. "I had not the faintest idea where the jewels came from. I only knew that in my palm I had at least a partial solution to my debts. I was a fool, I know that, but I sent Eturah first with the loose stone, and then with the ring to the Barrier. I meant to redeem them later when I had won back my losses; and I swear to you that I never once dreamed that there was any connection between those jewels and the murder and theft in the church."

Reilly rose heavily and looked at her with an icy smile. "I suppose, madam, that you hang up your stocking and Santa Claus comes down the chimney and fills it, and rabbits lay Easter eggs in your little nests, and you probably have a trained frog that opens it's mouth and drops out diamonds and rubies."

She went paler than ever. "I know it sounds fantastic—"

"Fantastic," repeated Reilly, "is crass understatement. Some unknown benefactor sends you jewels, you accept them without inquiry."

"Oh! Not without inquiry," she protested. "I did try to learn—" And she stopped in the midst of her explanation, confused. We all waited for her conclusion. There was none and I saw Reilly shrug his shoulders.

"Senator," he said, ignoring the woman, "you'll permit me to say that, incredible as you promised your story to be, this outreaches any possible stretch of my credulity. I may believe that storks bring babies and fairy godmothers turn pumpkins into coaches, but I don't believe in Uncle Sam's mailman that delivers stolen jewels to the wives of United States senators. And if they do, I think we'd better get Jim Farley to look into the case."

The senator walked around the table and again took his wife's hand. He led her quietly to the door and opened it for her. When she was gone he came back to the table and faced us with more calmness than I had expected. Undoubtedly his wife was in a tough spot; so why was he so apparently unmoved by this sweep of events?

"Gentlemen," he began with his usual preamble, "I think I know just why this incredible thing has happened."

We looked at him with sheer skepticism. "There are," he continued, "thousands and thousands of men and women in this country that would love nothing more than to see me ruined, discredited; a fallen public figure." I know we all knitted our brows in puzzled surprise. "Communists would explode with joy if I were hounded from public life. The Bund would laugh with glee. They hate me, they know what I mean to do to them. So suppose that the jewels were in the hands of some of my enemies; they mail two of them to my dear, but somewhat mislead wife, and she is held for theft and murder. Do you see? My whole tremendous work of investigating and bringing to justice these foes of democracy is wrecked and they go free."

"By golly!" said Karl, and I saw that Karl's amazement was mild compared with the sudden understanding that lighted Reilly's face.

"Senator," said the detective slowly, "I'd forgotten: you are the chairman of the Senate Committee for the Investigation of Anti-American Activities, aren't you?"

As if the whole nation didn't know and hadn't read of the drive he'd been making against Reds and Nazis alike, I think that in a flash we saw the ramifications of the plot. If the senator's wife were implicated in murder and theft, if her racing debt were exposed, if he were held up to public ridicule…

"Smart, smart," murmured Reilly and he was on his feet in a second. "That's all for the present, Senator," he said. "I don't say your wife is not still under heavy suspicion, but—" he waved the question aside "—I think there are bigger fish in this pond."

And in his intense relief the Senator even forgot to resent the fact that his wife was called a fish.

That evening the four of us, the priest, Reilly, Karl and myself, gathered in the priest's little parlour and talked gloomily of the events of the week. Fr. Tierney was plainly tired, clearly worried. Reilly felt himself up against something bigger than he first expected, something that grew more intricate, more dangerous. Karl was deep in sympathy with the poor priest. As for myself:

"Since," said I, "we all know that Fr. Tierney is not guilty—"

"Thanks for the kind assurance," said the priest, smiling wanly.

"I see nothing for it but Schwartz and the Bund. And it all ties in; Schwartz hates Goodspeed, the senator has publicly said he'd have the lot of Nazis on their heels before he's finished with them. Schwartz has the jewels and sends two of them to the senator's wife, she falls into the trap, Schwartz still has the bulk of the jewels but he has hung the senator so high that his work with the Anti-Nazi committee collapses, and with it goes reputation and his prestige."

The phone rang, and Fr. Tierney moved across the room to answer it. We used the interval of silence to light our cigarettes and shift comfortably in the rectory's uncomfortable little chairs. Fr. Tierney listened for a minute and then signaled us. We all strained intently but through the phone all we could catch was the whisper of a voice with a decidedly foreign accent…or was it merely the blurred sound of the phone?

Fr. Tierney's answers were short, monosyllabic. Then he said, "If you wish it, I shall ask them to leave."

A pause. Then, "I shall ask them to leave" and Fr. Tierney hung up the receiver. He came back to the table and under the strong light he looked pale and worried, more so than ever.

"Well?" demanded Reilly.

"Someone, wouldn't give his name, says that if I am alone he'll come and tell me who really is the robber and the murderer."

"A gag!" I blurted. "Just another of these crazy cranks that always have the solutions of murder cases.

"Leave you alone like that?" demanded Karl. "Not on your life!"

But Reilly was standing rubbing his fingers up and down the rough stubble on his face. "Let's go, boys," he said quietly. "Don't worry, Father. We'll hang around, watch the place, spot the chap."

Strangely enough the priest lifted his hand in protest. "After all," he said, "I am a priest and if this man wants to talk to me in confidence I'll see him alone."

We all looked at his determined face silently. There was no doubt that he meant it, and he was right. So we shook hands silently with him, set the hour of return for 10:30—it was then a little before eight o'clock—and set out into the darkness. A uniformed cop was walking up and down before the church. Each of us had personal business that we had been neglecting in the heat of the chase so we parted, agreeing to meet again at the appointed time.

I was the first to arrive at Fr. Tierney's; the others were almost on my heels.

"Well?" we demanded. The priest shook his head.

"Look here, Father," said the detective, "I know all about the seal of confession, but if you got any information that might help us—"

The priest laughed ruefully and ran his hand through his hair. "That's just the point," he answered. "Nobody came."

It was my turn to laugh. "What did I tell you? Never yet was there a murderer, but a hundred fanatics and cranks were right there with the solution."

Reilly looked grim. "That was no crank," he said. He turned to the priest. "You didn't recognize the voice, Father?"

The priest shook his head.

"Well," said the detective, "I did, and I'm amazed that you didn't, you two. Father hadn't heard it before. You listened to it at quite some length."

It was Karl that picked up the cue. "Lyndski!" he cried in sudden remembrance and I slapped my leg in agreement. The sergeant nodded grimly.

"Lyndski it was. He evidently knows a lot more than we learned from him and he was coming clean. Father, wait for us and if he comes before we get back pull your front curtain half way up and we won't disturb you, but if he's still at the Barrier..."

The three of us got into a taxi and careened the few blocks to the smoke shop. It was closed tighter than the police had ever closed it and all our pounding on the door brought nothing but hollow echoes and a slight swaying of a lighted lamp that hung from a long pendulous cord inside the outer office. We walked back in disgust and Reilly voiced his determination that, with the morning, we'd be back and have Lyndski by the heels.

The curtains of the rectory were down so evidently Lyndski was not there. Fr. Tierney admitted us and this time he had coffee brewing for us on the little kitchen stove. We sat together around the rough table, half expecting the phone or the doorbell to ring. We drank our coffee silently.

"Boy!" said the sergeant allowing himself only that mild oath. "When you make coffee, Father, it has a kick like a sawed off shotgun." He drained the cup to the dregs and sat holding the empty cup in his hands. In the bottom of the cup were a few grains of coffee. "Mind if I have another cup?" he asked. But before the priest could answer he had walked to the sink and was filling his cup with water. "Mother," he said, "always had a fit if we kids threw coffee grounds into the sink." And he walked to the back door of the kitchen, cup in hand, turned the key in the lock and flung open the door.

Into the room tumbled the coated figure of a man. He fell face down with a horrible thump. Karl was on his feet in a second and standing over him. I knew that something like sheer horror made my heart miss a beat. Even as we stood in frozen statuary, I saw Fr. Tierney give what I knew must be conditional absolution. And then in a simple impulse we were around the figure, gently turning it over.

"Dead," said the detective. "Dead as last year's grasshoppers."

"Ego te si fieri potest absolvo," muttered the priest again and the blank dead face of the man looked up into the light, his eyes wide open. On the detective's hand was blood from the back of the dead man's head.

"Lyndski," whispered Karl, mouthing the name we all knew.

"Poor fellow," said the priest.

"He was going to talk," said the detective slowly, "only someone knew it."

We didn't dare look at Fr. Tierney, for another dead man had literally fallen at his feet and he had been the only one around when the murder had happened. We wondered with horror in our hearts just what the newspapers would say when this ghastly story broke in the morning's headlines.

Chapter Six

Murderers, say the old axiom, always return to the scene of the crime and if thieves have, through exigencies of a quick getaway, been forced to hide their plunder they are bound to come back and look for it. So, quite aside from the temporary ban that the Church had slapped on little St. Surgius, the state was keeping a close eye on the vicinity of the little Greek Uniate parish. Reilly assured us that the police had combed the church from tiny basement to trophied bell tower and found not a sign of a clue nor a trace of the jewels. And all the while police patrolled the vicinity of the church keeping a constant and, I thought, rather obvious watch for the return of the guilty man.

When the dead body of Lyndski toppled into the priest's parlour, however, all the hounds of the city bayed their wildest. Papers that had treated Fr. Tierney with some degree of consideration now openly suggested that if the man were not a priest and the police department not so notably Catholic in personnel, the DA would be asking Fr. Tierney more than a few polite questions that followed the news of Lyndski's murder. And the priest looked paler and more harrowed as he faced the guilt of the second murder for he was, to all seeming, the most likely person to be suspected.

I think this is what led Karl Reinhardt to do the utterly foolish thing that he did. But since he handled this part of the investigation all by himself, perhaps it would be better if the adventure were told in his own words. I merely remark by way of prelude that, when Reilly and I heard the story from his lips, we looked upon him as one of the rarest chumps it has been our blessed privilege to know.

Karl's story:

"No doubt about it: I felt like a chump too, before, during and after my solo flight as a detective. With the fingers of the world pointing in increasing numbers at Fr. Tierney, I just had to take the steps I took, silly as they seemed, and futile as they were for the time being. Briefly, I didn't believe that the police had ransacked that church so carefully as they could and should, and some hunch nudged me into the belief that I could find things that they had missed; perhaps some essential clue; perhaps the jewels themselves. At any rate, when I heard from our good friend Sergeant Reilly that the police were withdrawing the police guard from the church, (even though the diocese still kept it closed to public worship) I felt that my chance had come, my hour for amateur sleuthing. I felt like an incipient Nero Wolfe.

Reilly and Pierre Anton and I had dinner together in a small restaurant on the edge of Chicago's loop, a place frequented by Italians and Chicagoans that know good food and appreciate low prices. Reilly hit out to track some information about the Barrier Smoke Shop: information about which he was remarkably secretive, though Pierre and I did our best to pump him. Pierre left for home, admitting that he was dead from lack of sleep during the preceding days and that he wanted nothing but a little quiet and rest. And I found myself alone and with the most wonderful opportunity for exploring that church by myself. So I announced that I thought I'd hit the mattress too, and we parted at the door of the restaurant.

Only after cutting slightly north in the apparent direction of home I swung back south and west, picked up a Blue Island car, and dropped off three blocks below the Church of St. Sergius. It was still only after eight o' clock; much too early for the prowling I intended to do, so I stopped in at the little neighborhood movie and watched through the gentle era of garlic and Jewish cooking, the adventures of a plush lady and hands-tough cowboy in a series of episodes that seemed pretty tame after the events that had occupied us during these fast feverish days.

When my watch read 10:30 I left the newsreels unrolling the world before the neighborhood and headed in leisurely fashion back toward the church. In the pocket of my coat was a chisel and a flash with fresh batteries and in my heart was the thrill of my first enterprise of this sort. Then things began to happen.

Two blocks from the church I bumped forcefully and vigorously into the last man on earth I wanted to meet. I pulled back in a hurry and tried to pass around him but Schwartz caught me by the arm. And I saw that under his light coat he was wearing his Bund uniform. The Bund cap stood out in the light of a nearby lamp post.

"Reinhardt," he said, and his voice was gruff and heavy with not quite smothered anger, "I have just come from a Bund meeting. I don't need to tell you that your name was mentioned, without enthusiasm. At that I put it mildly. If I were German like you—"

"I am an American citizen," I blazed back at him.

He shrugged. "Under Hitler, Germans are Germans whatever the land that shelters them. But as I was saying, if I were a German, like you and, like you, had tried to trick my countrymen, I should not be walking the streets of a city so late, alone." And he swung off into the night, leaving me just a little more limp than I care to confess, even to myself.

Another block unrolled under my still leisurely stride and I met my second unwelcome acquaintance. She was talking to some woman on the corner and, for a moment, I was sure that the second woman was the Countess. That seemed incredible, though, and as I came within closer seeing range, the second woman shot away down a side street and Maud Bulling Whitecliffe bore down upon me with her quick nervous strides.

For just a moment, what with Schwartz, the silhouette of the woman that might have been the Countess and now this fanatical social worker, I felt haunted. What fiendish luck put in my path three people that could be witnesses to the fact that I was around St. Sergius Church in the regions of eleven o'clock.

But Miss Whitecliffe was in no mood for conversation. She looked at me with a concentration of dislike and suspicion that lowered the temperature of my blood perceptibly, laughed rudely when I lifted my hat, and then strode off into the lower reaches of the almost deserted street.

And just ahead of me loomed the now too familiar façade of the church that was my objective. I shan't bore you with the retelling of my clumsy efforts to kill time before making my approach. My affected carelessness as I reached the shadows of the building, my quick little run—I fancy I learned that from the movie criminals—as I saw that the street was really clear. I ducked into the dense darkness that lay on the far side of the church, the side away from the little rectory. I know that I felt as clumsy as a gorilla in a conservatory; perhaps I was more deft than I seemed.

My plan was simple: I meant to pry open a window as far forward in the church as possible, into the little sanctuary, explore the church and test a half dozen little conjectures that I'd formed during the preceding days. I know that when I slipped my chisel under the window, I blessed the happy chance that made the hardware in this old church rusty and untrustworthy. For the window gave with one short click and I lifted it with the quiet expertness that would, I am sure, have done credit to the second story men's union local thirteen. One leg over the sill, the other, a pause to pull my raincoat out of reach of probable protruding nails, and I dropped to the floor. One sweep of my flashlight gave me general directions and I headed in complete darkness for the sacristy. There, I was absolutely sure, lay the key to the mystery, perhaps the jewels, certainly a clue that we all had missed.

I groped my way along the communion rail and into the sacristy. I closed the sacristy door carefully, shutting off the church and any possibility that my movements might be heard. And with recurrent flashes of my light, I began the most careful combing of everything in that narrow little room that once had been the vestry of a protestant minister. It was the world's most futile search. Either there never had been anything to find or the police had done a better job than I was willing to believe, for there was just nothing to justify my efforts. I remember wondering with a wry kind of amusement whether Philo Vance or Sherlock himself wouldn't have hit on a white feather that was the symbol of a secret society or gathered up a handful of dust that would have contained more information than fossil sand does under the eye of a paleontologist. My quest was for something bigger than that and I found—just nothing.

I know that, disappointed and disgusted, I leaned against the little vesting table and ran my hand over my eyes, the way one would do in a dark room. And as I did, I know that some strange, unclassified sense, some nervous apperception, told me that I was not alone in that church. No, I knew there couldn't be any one else in that stuffy little sacristy. But though I'd heard not the slightest sound I was absolutely sure that there was another person somewhere out there in the blackness that held the body of the church in captivity.

My first impulse was to throw open the door and flash my light around, but I remembered that I'd read somewhere that that was the finest way in the world to make oneself a target for a bullet. A man in the darkness had only to shoot at the light and it was curtains. But if I could not use my light I could use my ears, so with the greatest caution I could manage in defiance of the trembling of my nerves, I opened the sacristy door little by little and stood, all my powers gathered into a single sharp point of auditory attention. And there was no further doubt about it; the sounds were so slight that an occasional street noise blotted them in complete blackout. For the man, as he moves through space careful as he may be, creates some sounds around him utterly different from all other sounds in the world.

I waited, not knowing what to do. Then suddenly I heard, from up over my head, a click. It was followed by a low rumble that made my throat go dry and my fingers convulse in terror. But the instinctive reaction was relieved by the desire to laugh. Some one had turned on the electric switch of the organ in the loft in the back of the church and the automatic bellows were beginning their first mournful sigh, before they saw down to the business of feeding wind to the pipes. Laughter in turn dried in my throat. What crazy idea was this? In the darkness, in this church of murder and thievery somebody had come to play the organ by night.

I stood hardly breathing, following in imagination each step of the unseen organist. Would he turn on the light and show himself to me through the darkness? I felt rather than heard him open the cover of the manuals and slowly turn it back. I could imagine him slipping softly onto the organ bench. His foot struck an unexpected manual pedal and one short grunt broke the stillness. Quickly I argued. The man—or is it a woman?—is no organist. A skilled organist slides in and out without risking the slightest possibility of brushing the quickly aroused pedals. I seemed to feel the fingers grope in the darkness for the old-fashioned stops and I wondered whether he'd be organist enough to pick out soft stops, or would instead choose some loud blasting combination that would respond in a blaring sound.

I soon had my answer. Through the silence came the sound of a fumbled chord. Correct enough, but inexpert in the pressure on the keys. With only one hand the organist, man or woman, fumbled about and as he or she caught at the chords, I know I tried to associate this action with any of the characters in our drama. Schwartz came of a musical race; Germans. He might quite easily have had a bit of organ training as a boy. The Countess? Well, she had certainly learned the polite accomplishments of a noblewoman, of which music was one. Father Tierney? Yes, he had a key to the church and in the seminary undoubtedly an organ would have become familiar to him. As for Miss Whitecliffe, wasn't there the chance that a woman who managed a center, which among other things offered recreation of a sort, might know a trifle about basic chords?

One determination, however, was tightening the muscles in my throat. Somehow, I had to get into that choir loft. I had to turn on the light. I had to see who was fooling around with that keyboard. Conviction forced itself on me then, till I was certain that if I could see the face of that musician I'd see the face of the thief and murderer.

Scarcely daring to breath, I moved from the shadow of the sacristy into what appeared the deeper shadows of the church, then toward a narrow side altar that gave me the wall for my guidance, and back into the rear where the darkness was pitch black under the little choir loft. Back in the darkness the musician kept fumbling. Suddenly one of the pipes squeaked and instantly the music stopped. Again in the blackness the musician picked out his keys, and after a moment the pipe squeaked again. This time he held his finger lingeringly on the squeaking key, as if the ugly dissonance gave him some peculiar pleasure. Then silence again.

Soon, I had reached the foot of the narrow stairs that led up into the choir loft. I heard a slight movement of feet above my head. The musician was now walking quietly about the loft. Then again the fumbling for chords and the wheeze of that dissonant pipe, and I was well on my way, creeping noiselessly, bent until I was almost crawling on hands and knees up the steps. Above me I heard a peculiar scraping sound, then more footsteps, and, in my intensity, I gripped my flash as if it were a weapon. In fact, I was almost at the point now where my head was on a level with the floor of the loft and I turned the flash in the general direction of the scraping sound. In a moment, no doubt of that, I would look straight in the face of the person we wanted. I knew with all the intensity of my deepest convictions that that face would not be Fr. Tierney's. I pointed my flash, took a final step, felt with my thumb for the button that would throw the light and, suddenly, evidently one step was a trifle higher than the other, I hit my toe against the tread and plunged forward into the loft. Because I had been so tense and taut I fell hard, fell with a thudding *bang!* that seemed to wake a thousand echoes in the silent church. Painfully I arose, determined to fill the loft with light and learn the identity of the intruder. As I turned I heard a sharp breath behind me, and that was all.

The blow that lay me flat there on the choir loft floor was evidently swift, skillful and vindictive. And I was completely out, like a candle smashed into the hand of a giant.

That's my story and that's all I know. When I came to, there was what I thought to be a trace of light in the windows of the church. I was wrong. It was merely the reflection of an auto lamp that faded even as I looked. My watch in the darkness radiumed the hour: It was two o'clock, A.M evidently. I felt my head woefully and touched the bump with tender regret. Then I scuffled my feet around the floor until they touched the torch, which must've fallen out of my hand. I picked it up and turned it's white light in purposeful gestures around the loft, the empty church below, the staircase. There was less than nothing.

I went back to my window, climbed out cautiously and got a belated Al Taxi that took me home and to bed. At least I'd tried. I'd come closer to the solution than had any of the others, and I'd failed."

That's the story as Karl told it to Reilly and myself the next morning. I know that, as he told it, Reilly and I avoided each other's eyes. It was such a simple trick, such a purposeless one and the implications might make everything far, far worse for Fr. Tierney. It was such a stupid trick!

"Karl," I said, touching his arm gently for he was still a sick looking man with a goose egg giving a queer couture to the front of his head, "don't you see what a gosh awful thing you did?

Suppose you'd been caught. Nobody in the world would have thought you were anyone else but the thief going back to find his hidden swag." I saw from the grim line of Reilly's jaw that he had thought of that too.

Karl rubbed his goose egg ruefully. "That's an angle I didn't think of," he admitted. Then, he looked from one to the other of us almost wistfully. "I admit that I am a prize jackass," he said quietly. "But you don't really think that I'm the man you're looking for, do you?"

Reilly laughed shortly. "Karl," he said, "no matter what I say, it's bound to hurt your feelings. But I honestly think the fellow we want is a lot, lot smarter than you are. If you ever are arrested you can play incredible ignorance and extenuating stupidity." We all laughed in sharp relief.

Only fifteen minutes later Reilly had the two of us in a taxi once more and with an official warrant from headquarters, turned us toward the little church on Blue Island Avenue. Because of the events of the night Reilly had asked that a patrolman be put back on the job. A big, hearty copper waved at us when we presented our papers and inserted the key in the church door. Reilly swung it open and we followed him in.

"Looks a lot different from the way it looked last night," said Karl with a short laugh, and Reilly turned straight for the choir stairs.

"It's a very, very smart criminal that leaves no clues behind him," he said, "and I think we'll take a look."

The three of us in the little choir loft made the thing seem about the size of a collar-box and investigation was largely a matter of trying not to get in each other's way. I know that Karl was glad when Reilly told him to sit down and relax. I sat on the ledge of the railing and watched the detective as he went over that organ, the bench, the floor, the rail, with a thoroughness of a hungry hound disposing of a large smooth bone. He scratched his head thoughtfully as he finally stopped in the center of the choir, facing the organ. Then he bounded forward suddenly and gripped the music cabinet which stood slightly to the right. On the top of it was the usual disorderly pile of music that clutters all well-regulated choirs. But the pile was tipped crazily away toward the wall as if it had been tilted and thrown out of balance. Reilly's strong hands jerked the case from the wall and then he plunged his right arm down and back.

"Got it!" he cried eagerly, and I could see Karl thought he meant the missing treasure, for his face lighted and he was with Reilly in a single bound. Only it was no catch of jewels that Reilly pulled out from behind that dusty case. It was a Bund cap; clean and neat except for the brief contact with the whitewashed wall. Reilly held it in triumph.

"Schwartz," I cried. Here at last was a real clue! Reilly nodded grimly, and with stern satisfaction he reconstructed the scene of the night before.

"You met Schwartz on the street near the church, didn't you Karl?"

Karl nodded.

"He gave you time to get out of the way, broke into the church, much as you did; came up to the choir loft and tossed his hat on that stack of music. You disturbed him in whatever he was doing—recovering the jewels perhaps." Reilly interrupted himself to scan the tiny choir loft in puzzled anger.

"Not room here to hide a kid's first tooth," he said, interpreting his own look. And then he resumed the reconstructing.

"When he heard you he moved suddenly and jarred the pile of music, and his hat pitched back against the wall and slid out of sight. He hit you and didn't dare pause to look for his hat; that precious tell-tale cap. He was off and the smart criminal had made his one mistake."

I know we all felt the same thrill of satisfaction, but Reilly was all business. "Let's get 'im!" he cried, and poured the three of us down that short flight of stairs as if he were a human landslide slipping over a steep hillside.

Yes, the secretary said, Mr. Schwartz was in his office. Yes, she continued after a brief consultation on the phone, he'd see us. Reilly's nod meant that he'd better see us. Grasping a little more securely the newspaper in which he had sandwiched the Bund cap, he led us across the ante office and the secretary threw open the door to reveal Schwartz very busily occupied with papers at his large and expensive desk.

"Schwartz," barked Reilly in his best you'd-better-come-through-or-else voice, "We've a few questions to ask you."

Schwartz waved us to chairs with all the calm of a millionaire meeting a benevolent society committee's request for a donation. Only Reilly had no time for polished acting. He leaned across the desk his face close to Schwartz and said almost in a whisper, "How about a complete program of your activities last evening?"

Schwartz shrugged his shoulders. "And you talk of police interference in Germany," he sneered. "Well, I worked fairly late in the office, then walked home and along the way met your good friend here, Reinhardt. He'll vouch for that."

Reilly copied the sneer. "Correct. He found you very close to Saint Sergius Church." And Reilly hammered those last words with his voice and three blows on the polished desk. Schwartz shrugged again and continued.

"And I went home and slept peacefully, anticipating, I'm sure, some pleasant surprise in the morning. Even perhaps a visit from friends like you."

"And an alibi all arranged, I suppose?"

"Well, I was called to the phone, as is not unusual with me, three times between eleven and twelve o'clock. Those calls will be easy to check. And as one of the men is merely a business acquaintance, I think even the police may accept his evidence that I was home last evening when he called me."

"Why are you so insistent," pried Reilly, "on your whereabouts between eleven and twelve?"

The Bund leader flashed angrily.

"Because," he said, "after that I was in bed, asleep. Before that your friend can account for me. And anyhow it bores me to answer your impertinent questions. And I demand to know by what right—"

Reilly hit a sense of the dramatic and from out of his folded newspaper he whisked the Bund cap. Like a magician climaxing his best trick, he thrust it under the Bundster's nose.

"Because you may be interested to know where I found that."

Either the man was a magnificent actor, I thought, or his conscience was that of a babe in arms. He merely looked at the hat for a second then, through slightly glinted eyes, turned his gaze on the detective.

"Frankly," he said, "I don't care where you found it."

"Then I'll tell you anyhow, and see how you take it. That hat was found by us three this morning in the church of St. Sergius. It's clean so it's not been there long. And last night—but I'm sure you know more about last night than any of us do. Now will you tell us where you were last evening and what you were doing, or shall I take you and your Bund cap straight to headquarters?"

"*My* cap?" Schwartz stressed the pronoun in flat insult. With a quick gesture he took the cap in one hand and with a forefinger of the other pressed a button. Instantly the secretary appeared.

"Bring me," said he, and he flipped back the sweatband of the cap and looked inside, "files of uniforms from 20,000 to 21,000."

We stood silent at this unexpected twist in the business. In a flash the secretary was back and laying on his desk a locked folder. His key opened it, his thick finger ran down the list, his nervous eye compared what he found on the paper with markings on the inside of the cap. Then:

"I have not too much respect for the American police," he said in heavy insult. "This is not my cap," and he held it out to Karl. "This cap belongs to your precious friend here."

And he flung the cap to Karl who instinctively caught it.

"Now if you'll please relieve me of this annoying, boring visitation…"

Chapter Seven

Sometimes I had an unhappy feeling that Sgt. Reilly was working more and more by himself on our desperate case. I could not get over the sickening notion that he lumped Fr. Tierney and Karl with the other possible suspects. And this in spite of the fact that the priest and the young organist were our good and trusted friends. As for Karl, I worried because he, too, seemed to be heading off for himself. We saw less of him. We felt that he wasn't taking us into his confidence anymore. He looked more tired than even the pressure of worry might explain, and he avoided Fr. Tierney almost altogether. Yet we did reassemble in the priest's little parlor, the four of us, to sift what trifles we had recently gathered in the now obviously stalling quest. Reilly shuffled the mental cards and laid them out before us.

"The list of possibles is really pretty limited."

"Unless someone we don't know, haven't even met, someone who blundered in and stumbled on the jewels…" I began.

Reilly thrust the suggestion aside with disgust. "There is no stranger in this," he said. "Whoever did it knew about the jewels and we know everyone who knew. Whoever did it knew that Father here had them in his possession; knew something of the habits of that unlucky sacristan."

We agreed readily enough, though we hated to admit the possibility of his theory. For by admitting that, we were drawing the circle too closely around the few who may be involved. Reilly was summarizing again. "Even though he slipped out this time, Schwartz is high up on the list. I'll admit that the senator's explanation makes the whole business of the way his wife got the jewels sound less fishy, but yet—"

"Could the Jap himself…" Karl began in tentative questioning.

Reilly looked thoughtful again. "Headquarters tracked down what they could find of his record—just nothing." He paused and scratched his blue-black stubble with a tough finger nail. Then he jumped to his feet. "By golly!" he said softly. "That's a possibility. Karl, phone Professor Jones at the university." Karl looked bewildered. "He's head of the department of Japanese literature,"

Reilly explained. "Ask him to drop around at headquarters in…two hours." Reilly jumped up and grabbed the priest's phone, shouting into it the well remembered number of police headquarters. "Reilly speaking. I'll have some films, perhaps in two hours. I'll want them developed immediately. Have the darkroom ready." He hung up the phone and grabbed his hat.

"If any of you are interested—"

"We'll be there," I answered for Karl and myself. Then I added, half humorous, "headquarters in two hours."

Reilly almost rushed into the police laboratory in his excitement. Professor Jones was sitting placidly reading a detective story which I thought a touch, with living detectives around him—maybe fiction is more exciting than life. The police officer from the identification bureau was waiting, a rubber laboratory apron in his hand. Reilly emptied his pockets and shot the contents in various directions.

"Professor," he said, "If you'll just see whether you can read these…" and he tossed the professor a bundle of envelopes containing a thin rice paper that is used for most Japanese correspondence. In the direction of the laboratory policeman he volleyed three rolls of film carefully wrapped in the familiar red jackets. "And get those developed—but not printed—immediately."

The Professor retired to the inner sanctum of his own soul. The laboratory specialist disappeared and Reilly took off his hat and wiped his sweaty brow.

"That Jap!" he muttered, and then, addressing the world at large, "I'd as soon try to cross-question a freshly caught codfish, but I got him in the end…or I *hope* I got him." He paused ruefully, as if he were far from sure of himself.

"What's in those letters?" I demanded. "And why the film?"

Reilly looked up in mock despair. "If I knew, would I be calling in experts? Maybe something, maybe nothing but a joke on me. And when he answered me in that double talk that makes the Japanese such a chummy commutative race I suddenly sprang a search warrant and believe me or not, he actually helped me search his belongings and he was amused when I took the letters and film. Positively amused."

The professor looked up from the mess of rice paper. "Whoever your Japanese friend is, (and his name doesn't seem to be quite correct Japanese,) he's a nobleman; has connections with people in high places and is here in the States on government business."

Reilly slapped his thigh delightedly. "Wrong, Professor! He admits he's only a poor sort-of butler."

The professor turned back to the letters with a sage nod. "I've heard of important Japanese before who were glad to be just butlers…" his voice trailed off. "If they could serve in the right houses."

So that was that, I thought. Or rather that was just the beginning of something new and important and significant. With Japan and Russia at each other's throats and Japan knowing of these Russian jewels…

The laboratory specialist returned, trailing behind him a long black snake of damp film. "A rush job," he said, "and I'll have to wash them some more, but—listen, Reilly; you're wasting your time." He held the film up to the light. "Not even pictures. Just a lot of scratches like the kind I get on my laundry."

"Dry 'em," commanded Reilly, "and fast."

And he began to push buttons and summon people until we had a projector set up. Then the films came back, now dry, and they were thrown on the small screen. We all leaned forward in our chairs while the professor spilled out the crawling worms of letters with surprising fluency. As far as the murder and the theft were concerned, not a thing did those films mean. As far as a our good friend Eturah Najoki was concerned, they meant plenty. For those films were instructions to an espionage chief who, it seemed, was in constant communication with subordinates who were too close to our arsenals and navy yards for the comfort of the United States. Then, at the very end, the professor sprang the surprise.

"Funds," he read in the toneless voice of a translator, "are painfully low. We cannot long hide this from ourselves or from the nation. If at Russia's cost or the cost of any of our other enemies you can obtain funds, money for munitions, decimating our mounting debt—" The professor stopped.

"Go on!" I cried breathlessly.

"That's all," said the professor.

"Do we need any more?" demanded Reilly. "I'd say the professor has read enough to hang on our Jap a motive that—"

Ah, I thought ruefully, *but that's precisely the trouble. There are too many people; too many motives. Too much everything in fact, except a nice tangible thing like a clue, a murderer, or the missing jewels.*

Karl left us soon after this and was gone for the rest of the afternoon. Just before six o'clock, however, my phone rang and it was Reilly. He was having dinner with Karl. Would I join them? As fast as the elevator could manage it, I was with them and our problem was again hanging heavy over our heads. Only when we had reached desert did Karl take over the discussion.

"This time," he said, "I'm not going to play the fool again. I may be crazy, but I'd prefer to be crazy with a couple of other fellows."

"Meaning us?" I asked.

"With whom else would I share my delightful insanity?" he demanded, and we both bowed our ironic gratitude. "We're going back to the church tonight," he said as calmly as if he'd announced that we were going out to see the Marx Brothers at a neighborhood movie house. "All three of us. As I say, I may be simply mad but if I'm not…"

Mad or not we were with him and when the evening was dropping quietly into night, we presented our papers to the policeman doing sentry duty outside the church and followed Reilly into the dark interior.

"Wait," said Reilly, "until I turn on the lights." Only there weren't any. Reilly clicked the switch up and down with no results other than the sharp sound through the thick darkness. Evidently the electricity had been turned off. Reilly produced his flash and muttered grimly to himself about the joy of working in unlighted buildings.

"And getting beaten over the head," I added cheerfully.

He flashed off his light to save the batteries and in the darkness he said, almost querulously, "Karl, I think it is about time we stopped playing fraternity initiation and you told us what it's all about."

Karl steered us into a back pew. "Sit," he commanded. "Now if I may have the flash." I thought that I could feel Reilly hesitating only so slightly before he handed it over. Maybe Karl felt it, maybe not. At any rate he said, "If you'd feel more comfortable with your gun in your hand, Reilly …" and the sergeant growled again.

"If you'll be patient just a moment," Karl said, and with a quick leap, the white circle of the flash convoying him, he was up the dark stairs. I heard him snap the organ switch but nothing happened. The juice that fed the lights fed the electric motor too. The muffled sound from the choir loft might have been an oath. At least Reilly cried out in mock horror, "Not in church, Karl, not in church!"

Then I heard the unmistakable sounds of someone prowling around the choir loft. Then a pleased exclamation from Karl, and his voice calling us.

"This was not originally an electric organ," he said. "The old fashioned hand pump is still here. You fellows come up and help me." We were up the stairs in three bounds and Karl gestured toward the handle of the pump which was thrust out like an exaggerated dog tail.

"Pump!" commanded Reilly. "I never was good at music." I caught the wheezy pump handle and slowly moved it up and down. Karl moved a few of the stops experimentally, then he touched a single note. It sounded soft and mellow, even against the scraping of the ancient bellows. Then quietly, Karl matched that single note with a grouping of chords, playing them tentatively; experimentally. It was a lovely fullness that sounded warm and comforting in the darkness. And all the while Reilly kept the white circle of his flash like a spotlight on the man at the organ.

Slowly, Karl moved the successive modulation of the chords up the keyboard. All of a sudden a single high squeak came from the organ. As suddenly, Karl jerked his fingers from all the other keys and as if to drive us mad with the wailing of that false tone he kept his finger pressed on the controlling key. "B flat, second octave below middle C," he said. And then without warning he ran a chromatic scale from the middle of the keyboard up to the very top, then he reversed the direction of his skillful fingers and ran the scale downward to the very last note.

Only once did the ancient organ squeak in protest and that was when, somewhere in the mid-bass, that single note was hit.

"If you ask me," said I, stopping my actions at the pump, for the exertion was beginning to make me perspire, "I've heard you do lots better. Let's go where we can get a good organ, and then you can really give us a concert."

For once Karl was rude and abrupt. "Keep pumping," he ordered. And then to Reilly, "Where's that screwdriver I told you to bring?"

Reilly fished the parts of a screwdriver out of his pocket and jointed them together.

"Press down on the pump," Karl cried, and his expert fingers again picked out the discordant note. "Here, Reilly," he commanded. "Put your finger on that." Reilly obeyed in a kind of daze and laid his heavy, stocky finger gingerly on the yellowish-white key. Instantly, Karl was off the bench and hauling a plain wooden chair toward the organ. "Keep pumping hard," he commanded. "Don't let go of that key." As he passed the keyboard, he pulled out another handful of stops that swelled the volume until that horrible out-of-tune note simply wined and shrieked and yelled at us. I thought I couldn't stand the noise when my attention was sharply caught by the strange actions of Karl. With that screwdriver he was working at the ornamental pipes in front of the organ. "False pipes, of course," he said. "All cheap organs are built like that. Keep pumping!" he cried. Then he put his head close to the pipes that showed up within. "Your flash," he demanded of Reilly, "and hold onto that key." Then in a second, "I've got it! Stop pumping. Reilly, your music lesson is over. Turn the flash on me while I work. Hold it steady." With that screwdriver he dug out the big screws that held the base pipe. Then he cried, "catch it." The pipe began to sway in our direction. The last screw was almost out, but Karl didn't wait to remove it entirely. He wrenched out the pipe, dragging it out of place and tipped it in his arms.

Out of the interior, into the white light of the flash slid a slow, brilliant, dazzling rain of stones that dropped into the outstretched hands of Reilly, and then into the hat that I held under the gentle but stupefying flow. There must have been fully ten of the gems. At first Reilly was speechless with delight. Then he was overcome with the realization that we'd only part of the loot.

"Where's the rest?" he demanded. Karl caught the flash out of his hands and worked behind the pipes. He pulled out more jewels, and more, and more.

"If it hadn't been," he explained as he worked, "that that one pipe caught some of the jewels as they were tossed into the organ we'd not have known they were here. They'd have lain there until the thief came to look for them himself."

"How in thunder did you know?" demanded Reilly.

Karl, who had now sunk down upon the bench in relief and happiness, dusting the dirt of the ancient organ off his hands, laughed in weariness and triumph of his discovery. "I should have guessed it the other night," he said, "when the fellow—or woman—was working up here. That squeak meant that something had got in the pipe, and whoever was playing the organ was looking for that squeak. He ran the keyboard again and again until he got the right note. Then in the darkness I heard scraping. That was when he or she went to work on the pipes. Only, well, I was a thick-head or else that goose egg on my sconce knocked whatever sense I had out of it—until this evening."

Reilly turned the flash in the hat, my hat, full of jewels. He balanced them in his hands. And then he looked up in cynical disgust. "Frankly," he said, "though this is fine, I'd rather—a lot rather—have my hands on the murderer and thief." Reilly had the jewels, but what good were they? They did not prove the innocence of Fr. Tierney, indeed the fact that they were hidden in his church might be new reason for suspecting him. Karl, well, Karl had helped find them but on the other hand, if Karl had hidden them first and then fearing that the situation was growing too hot, he merely "discovered" what he knew all the time was there…As for the others, now that the jewels were found there was less chance than ever of finding the murderer and thief. I knew just how tricked Reilly felt. He had the motive for the crime, he didn't have the criminal who had snuffed out two lives to gain these jewels.

I leaned against the rail, looking out into the darkness of the church. Reilly sat silent, his heavy shoes beating against the base of the organ bench. Karl took a turn up and down the loft.

Reilly grumbled deep in his chest. "What good are these things? Not even a decent reward for them. I'd rather—a thousand times rather—we'd never see the things again, if only we could lay by his heels the man—"

"...Or woman," I insisted. Then Karl snapped his fingers and laughed aloud. I knew that the created fever that was on him had had a gratifying result.

"Well?" demanded Reilly.

Karl talked fast. "If the jewels were no longer in the organ, we'd have not the slightest chance of finding the murderer. But if the jewels were replaced, if we stood guard over them, let the murderer and thief know that we suspected where they were and that we meant to go for them, he or she would try to beat us to them and in the act would give himself away."

Reilly sat for a second in profoundest thought. Then he was on his feet with a thump that shook the ancient choir loft. He held out the hat full of jewels to Karl. "I'm a fool," he said, "and I may lose my job for this, but I believe you're right. Stick 'em back exactly the way we found 'em."

It was harder, we found, to replace an organ pipe than it was to rip it out. But Karl knew organs and he handled that screwdriver with a skill I'd never have suspected in those musically trained fingers.

While Karl was working, Reilly was giving voice to his doubt. "Aren't we actually giving the thief another chance at the jewels? Suppose he outsmarts us. Suppose he gets the jewels and gets away with them. How could we ever explain to the authorities that we actually had the jewels in our hands and then put them back into the organ as bait for the thief, who may be smart enough to get them and never even flick his lower lip on the hook we are baiting so carefully?" But he was determined to go ahead. He left us inside the church while he made a few routine calls. When he came back we drew lots to see which one would take the first stretch guarding the jewels.

"No watch necessary, really," said Reilly, "before late tomorrow afternoon. By that time we'll get the word to all the suspects and then it's a sleepless guard till the thief's nervous anxiety to get his jewels puts him right in our hands." Then he almost jumped with the suddenness of his idea. "Hold everything! Along with the hint that we're on the trail of the jewels we'll send out the hint that the church is being freed from police guard because nothing suspicious has been found there. That plants the fear that the jewels may be found yet removes the fear of capture in the church itself."

So the reporters found Reilly uncommonly communicative when around midnight they stopped him and demanded some news. The morning papers announced in splash headlines that the police were hot on the trail of the missing jewels and that the guard at the church of St. Sergius had at last been completely lifted by the police.

We agreed, we three, to keep four hour vigils. I was to watch from eight o'clock to midnight, Reilly from midnight until four, Karl from four until eight. During the day a plainclothes man in the vicinity would be guard enough. Reilly had us sworn in as deputy sheriffs and presented each of us with a badge and gun, which, truth to tell, gave us a considerable thrill. After dinner I set off for my first spell of sentry duty, entered the locked church by the window that Karl had previously opened, and settled down in the back pew. I did manage to stay awake, and dull business it was. At midnight Reilly entered the window and took over and I went home. We met the following noon with nothing to report, and the following noon we had even less. On the third night, my watch was as eventless as the life of a marooned sailor on an uninhabited island in the Pacific. So with real relief I gave my watch over to Reilly. Just for luck we tested the organ and found it had been untouched. I left the church as I had entered it, through the window. It was a little after nine o'clock in the morning when my phone's insistent ring pulled me up short. I answered sleepily and in considerable disgust. For as much as I hate telephones, I hate them most when they substitute for an alarm clock. Then I jumped to attention. It was Reilly.

"Get down here fast," he said, and I knew it was urgent. "I'm in Providence Hospital. Come up to room 339," he ordered and he clicked off.

I think a new record was established between my apartment and Providence and another one between the hospital lobby and 339. Reilly's voice answered my knock, and I entered to find Reilly and another detective standing against the wall. In the bed, his head bandaged and his right eye a villainous mass of colors, lay Karl Reinhardt, too sick apparently to care who came or went in his room.

"Karl!" I cried, and then turning to Reilly with a quick grasp of what had happened, "They're gone?"

Reilly nodded grimly. I didn't care that Karl looked like death's younger brother, I dashed to the side of his bed and cried, pressing his hand, "I don't believe you did it. No one can persuade me you did." Karl opened his eyes wearily. He grinned and pressed my hand in return.

"Twice is pretty often," said Reilly, in what I thought needless cruelty, "but maybe you'd like the hear his story." I turned angrily on Reilly.

"If you don't mind," I said, "I'd rather leave a sick man in peace. Would you mind detailing someone to go with me to the church?" Reilly leaned against the wall. "Come on," he said, then barking at the other detective, "Settle down and make yourself comfortable. You'll be relieved around noon." In the taxi that raced across town Reilly unbent enough to tell the version of the story. Karl it seems, claimed that around five or six o'clock he fell asleep—"Which, of course, was most convenient," footnoted Reilly—then, next he knew, daylight was streaming in the window and he had a bump on his head that made the other goose egg feel like a slight pimple. When he staggered out of the church, the plainclothes man who took over at 8:00 spotted him, caught him just as he was falling, rushed him off to Providence. "Karl claims all he knows is that he's a mighty, mighty sick young man, and I know he has an awful lot to explain."

We piled out of the taxi in front of the church and bolted in. Fr. Tierney was kneeling in the back saying his Office. He got up when we entered. "You might," he said, "have let me in on the fact that you had actually found the jewels."

"And how do you know we found the jewels?" demanded Reilly, suddenly dramatically tough. The priest didn't deign to answer. He merely watched us as we climbed up the stairs to the organ loft, and it was a mess. This time there was no question of there having been a delicate handling of a screwdriver. The whole front of false pipes was ripped out and the base pipe that had held the tell-tale jewels, lay on the floor where it had been carelessly tossed. Not so much as a single small garnet of the cash of jewels remained.

"All clear," said I, "but how can a man knock himself out? Karl is a sick, sick man. Do you mean to tell me that he beat himself over the head?"

Reilly looked his contempt. "An old gag," he said, and he trotted down the stairs, I after him. A window far in the back of the church was wide open. From under a pew where he had evidently hidden it, Reilly pulled out a hammer tied by a string to a brick. "We found this outside the window on the ground. S.S. Van Dine used this trick in one of his stories. But it's all good; victim hangs his brick outside the widow, sits near the window, bangs himself on the head with a hammer, passes out like a light and drops the hammer. The brick pulls the hammer out of the window and is picked up by the supposed victim later on." I looked amazed, but Reilly stopped and look intently at the floor. "Only," he said, "This time the victim didn't retrieve the hammer. Its funny, I wonder why he didn't."

Chapter Eight

I think it was the very fact that Reilly had, from the start, been sure who the guilty man was that he made him do what he did. Perhaps Fr. Tierney was also implicated in the sorry mess. I could see why, needing money as he did for the work he meant to do in Russia, he might be tempted to inveigle Karl into the plot that climaxed when the unexpected interference of Radolf, the sacristan, brought on the ghastly murder. But at all events, Karl was clearly in the thing up to his neck and only the barrier of an ugly rope could stop it's rising. I don't like to think of death and death for a friend.

At any rate, we left the church together, Reilly and I, and we walked slowly down Blue Island Avenue. Reilly didn't talk and I didn't want to. Finally, Reilly said, "I'm having a round up of a lot of the suspects. I'm picking them up on, oh, any of a half dozen charges. We're taking them all to headquarters…No, we'll take them to Providence Hospital. Somehow, in that little room of Reinhardt's I'm going to get the truth out of them."

"All the suspects?" I demanded, for through my mind flashed the long list: Fr. Tierney, the Countess, Miss Whitecliffe, the senator's wife, that Japanese butler who was an espionage agent, Schwartz, Karl—

"All of them," he answered, and we let it go at that. I left him at headquarters. And since I had some business of my own that I had shamefully neglected, I was off to care for it with the understanding that we'd meet again in the lobby of Providence Hospital that evening at 8:00.

"I'll have them all there," Reilly said grimly. "Though whether it will do the least good, I don't know."

I shook his hand sadly. "Listen, Reilly," I said, not minding the fact that what I said would sound a little on the sentimental side, "if the guilty person does turn out to be Fr. Tierney or Karl, don't be surprised if I blow town for a while. I just couldn't stand it if those two friends of mine…"

He gave my hand a little extra pressure that showed that he did understand.

There is a little reception room that opens off the main parlour of Providence Hospital. Ordinarily it is reserved for doctors who want to sit and talk, but the Sisters had turned it over to Reilly and I joined him there.

Through the half closed doorway we could watch the slow assembly of the strange people who had been brought together in the circle of this crime. Miss Whitecliffe came first, looking down her nose contemptuously at the nun who ushered her into the parlour and thanking her with a phrase that sounded like an icicle dropping on the surface of a frozen lake. She inspected the parlour with critical disapproval and perched on a chair, sitting on the edge with her hands tightly folded and her lips one thin line of white flesh.

The Sister who ushered Fr. Tierney in was full of regrets about the sad events that had marked the beginnings of his work as a priest. But, she assured him, in all sincerity, a priest who began with so terrible a trial would undoubtedly be blessed by God. At which Miss Whitecliffe pulled in her breath so emphatically that she sounded like a vacuum cleaner biting on a particularly tough piece of grit. Schwartz walked in in military fashion, saluted the priest with an uplifted hand and stood with his back rigidly against the wall. The little Jap slipped into the room noiselessly and unobtrusively, as if he really were a butler instead of the nobleman we knew him to be. Senator Goodspeed came with his wife. The whole business was obviously profoundly distressing to him, yet clearly he had no alternative but to come and pray a gentle Providence that reporters would be absent or blind.

The Countess arrived in a swirl of unseen sables. Somehow she always suggested sables, no matter what she happened to be wearing. This time it was a quite modest suit with no suggestion of richness about it. The men all stood honouring her beauty and she acknowledged the greetings with an aloof, weary bow. I was a little amazed when the last man to enter was Mel Clineman whom I knew through our experiences at the Barrier Smoke Shop.

Reilly let them stew in their own nervous suspense before he signaled me quietly, and with a quick jerk threw the door wide open. They all turned toward him as if they had been jerked by strong though invisible strings. As I slipped to the side he closed the parlour doors and spoke briefly.

"I don't need to tell you, any of you, why you are here. Before you leave, I am going to know something that one, or perhaps two of you know. You may as well be told now as later that I already have learned far more than the wisest and cleverest of you suspect. We need a few last items and our case is complete."

Schwartz looked over the crowd with a twisted sneer. "These police!" he said. "Everywhere they are such wonderful actors and such wretched doers."

I watched the Countess rise slowly, all her languid charm turned on for the benefit of the men present. "It is distressing. None of this save the return, please the good God, of my jewels can concern me. Still…"

Reilly flung open the door that led into the hall. "Come," he commanded, and as he led us toward the stairs I noticed that from nowhere in particular two plainclothes men had come to take up the rear. No one was going to slip away unnoticed. Deliberately Reilly avoided the elevator and led us to the stairs. At the first landing the senator was puffing slightly. The unaccustomed walk up the second flight caused the Countess to hold her heart ostentatiously. Schwartz, who suddenly began to dance attendance upon her, took her arm. She smiled faintly and gently shook him off.

Room 339 was closed. We paused before it until our whole party was assembled, then Reilly laid his hand on the doorknob. "You will," he said, "find it a little congested in here." The word struck me as a crass understatement. "But if what I expect from you moves with dispatch…" He flung open the door and took one step. Then he fell back as if in complete surprise. And surprise it was! For as I craned over the startled heads of the assembled suspects, I too saw what he had seen and it amazed me. In the bed lay no sick man but a man dressed for the street even to his hat. Only he was not resting there calmly; he was squirming and tossing under the bondage of the white sheets that had been twisted into the ropes that held him tight. As Reilly dashed into the room and flicked on the full light, I saw that the man was the detective who, that morning, had been left to guard Karl Reinhardt. He was gagged and bound and fastened to the bed. But of Karl there was no slightest trace, except an opened window that led onto a fire escape.

It took only a minute for Reilly to slip the gag out of the hapless detective's mouth and cut the sheets that held him captive. The rest of us crowded in the doorway, knowing in a flash what this meant. It was as plain as if Karl had written his confession and left it pinned to the pillow. The others knew this too and I could feel a rush of exhausting yet exhilarating relief sweep through them. Reilly turned. "Back to the parlour, please; all of you…except you," he said, courteously thinking of me even in that emergency. He signaled the detectives who, like faithful sheep dogs, were herding the crowd down the corridor. Then he slammed the door and sat on the bed, looking at the detective, who, disheveled and furious, towered above both of us.

"Well?" Reilly demanded. "What happened? Tell us quick."

The detective fairly spluttered his story. But in spite of his irate confusion and indignation the thing was clear enough. Karl had pretended to be far sicker than he really was so the detective had relaxed his guard. His chair propped against the door, he even dozed a bit while Karl lay in an apparently genuine coma. Finally Karl had asked him for a drink. He gave it to him, leaning far over the bed and even lifting the sick man's head in an effort to relieve the apparent weakness. The next thing the startled detective knew a pillow slip was over his head and a rap hit him full on the chin. Before he could yell, Karl had hit him with something.

"The telephone," said Reilly, picking up the heavy continental phone and balancing it.

And when the detective regained consciousness he was lying gagged and tied in bed.

"How long ago?" demanded Reilly. The detective was rather vague. Evidently his coma had been something more like a sleep; he thought it might have been two hours.

"Come on!" said Reilly and he sprinted for the door. I followed him, glad that he still included me, regretful that I might have to be in on the capture of my friend. The suspects were all gone by this time and when we reached the ground floor the murmur of voices told us that they had once more been herded into the parlour. I thought that Reilly would head for the street; instead he sharply veered off toward the parlour, I still on toe, and entered, banging the door behind him. The group, which had been thrown into conversation by the community of their surprise and relief, stopped speaking and stood facing him expectantly.

"Ladies and gentlemen," said Reilly, his face somewhat purple from embarrassment, "policemen in the interests of their duty sometimes have to do strange and annoying things. I have caused you all considerable trouble during these last few days." Miss Whitecliffe's snort was loud in agreement. "But I assure you that now we definitely know the culprit."

Fr. Tierney burst out in protest. "I know it's not Karl!" he cried, "Believe me, it's not he. There is some explanation for his running away." He turned to me. "Pierre," he pleaded, "You *know* he's not guilty." I took his hand silently and shook it. Reilly watched him cynically. "Frankly," he said, "I may as well tell you, Fr. Tierney, that I am not sure he has been alone in this. And if it turns out—" I heard the Countess gasp. She was looking straight at the door which had opened so quietly that none of us had heard it. We all turned, impelled by her gasp. There in the doorway with his head still bound in blood-stained bandages, but with his street clothes on and a suitcase in his hand, stood Karl Reinhardt.

"Karl!" cried the priest.

"Grab him fast!" The detective barked it but short though the order was, his two assistants had closed in on Karl before it was finished.

Karl smiled at them and said, "That's alright, buddies. I have not least intention of running away." And shaking them off with a convincing gentleness, he walked across the room to the little table that stood with geometric precision in the very center of the parlour. All the while my eyes were on that suitcase. I knew his luggage and this was not his. It must have been absurdly light, if one could judge from the way a man whose sickness had been only partly faked was swinging it.

"Rally 'round," he said, and he turned toward the expectant group. "This is just a little surprise that I have for all of you." Then as we all pressed forward, he opened the suitcase and, flinging to right and left the loosely crumpled newspapers that filled the grip, pulled out a cigar box and then a second cigar box.

With maddening delay he broke the strings that bound them and poured onto the center of the table *the missing jewels!*

It is simply impossible to describe the expressions that followed this dramatic gesture. Everyone stood with his eyes riveted on that pile of precious stones for which one man, or perhaps two men, had died. I saw the detective near the door pull his gun and hold it loosely against his side. He knew what the sight of jewels did to the greedy human heart.

"They're mine!" suddenly screamed the Countess, all the veneer of culture falling from her, and stood over them as if to protect them from even the eyes of the others. Reilly pushed her aside, rudely, roughly. "They belong to the State until a lot of things are proved." He turned to Karl and there was venom in his voice. "It won't do you a bit of good," he said, in a low, penetrating voice, "turning back the jewels when we have you cornered isn't going to get you out of the double charge." He lifted his voice, "In the name of the Law, I arrest you for the murder of Radolf and Lyndski. And I warn you that anything you say may be used against you." Again the others gasped and I saw the flash of steel handcuffs as Reilly brought them from his pocket.

"Just a minute," said Karl as smoothly and coldly as if he had been invited out for a cheese on rye and a cool beer. "This isn't over yet. I'm willing to go along, Reilly, if you'll prove I'm guilty. But," and he swept the assembled group with his eyes, "there is one person here who knows I didn't do it and I'm going to ask that person to speak up to prevent an innocent man going to jail."

I saw Fr. Tierney start; for myself, I looked straight at Karl. It was the kind of thing you might have expected a devout Catholic like Karl to do; let himself seem to be the criminal to shield his priest and then at the end lose his nerve and ask the priest to confess.

Reilly shook his head angrily. "I've had enough of this nonsense, Reinhardt," he said. "Briefly, the case against you is so clear I need hardly repeat it. You were found in the church with the dead man, you were out of the house and in reach of Lyndski when he came to tell on you; you are an organist and would think of an organ as a place to hide the jewels. You pretended to be knocked out in the church and found the trick so good that you tried it the second time when you planned *really* to make away with the jewels.

You are the one who suggested putting the jewels back into the organ and I fell for your gag. Fell for it and gave you a chance to go and get the jewels during your own night watch! The brick and hammer trick has been tried too often to be anything but old stuff. Now that we have all this piled up against you, you are able to produce the jewels. You, who stole them in the first place and hid them, and stole them again! Now that things are too hot for you, you try turning them back and to top it all, this drama of trying to pin the thing on one of the others. No go, Karl! Hold out your hands for the cuffs."

Karl looked the crowd over again, this time almost beseechingly. "I tell you all, I'm innocent. You are not going to let this happen to me, are you? Won't the guilty one of you confess?"

"I—" Fr. Tierney began.

Karl shot at him with almost savage speed. "Shut up, Father!" He slowly walked around the room, looked quietly at each in succession. They winced or turned their eyes away or outstared him or shook their heads in angry or sorry protest; but none made the least sign of confession. At last he came to me.

"Goodbye, Pierre," he said quietly. "I'm sorry."

I took his hand. "I'm sorry too," I said, very close to tears.

"When I'm gone," he went on, "you can have your suitcase back."

"What are you talking about?" I demanded, and I felt the hot blood rush to my face.

He walked over to the table, closed the suitcase, and held it out to me. From the top stood the letters: **P.A.** "Your suitcase, Pierre," he said. And then turning to Reilly, he said very quietly, "I'm sorry I have to do this, Sergeant, but if you move fast you can lay your hands on the murderer and thief we're looking for—Pierre Anton."

I don't know what happened in those next few minutes. I only know that something inside me broke. I didn't laugh at him and defy the charge. The utter unexpectedness of the whole thing threw me completely off my normal, calm balance. I struck out at Karl, I lashed out at Reilly, and I plunged for the door in escape.

Only the detective in the doorway tripped me; I fell forward on my face. They were on top of me. Me! Who knew that if I could have kept my head and not let the utter surprise of the thing betray me into one false step I'd have bluffed them out. Instead I now have to sign my name to this, my confession.

But let me tell you that I *almost* succeeded. I almost succeeded in pinning the murder on that contemptible God-loving priest who had set himself to go back and sell the opium of religion to my fellow countrymen in the glorious, Godless Soviet. I almost had by the throat Schwartz and his filthy band of Nazis who are making war on communism and shutting up in their concentration camps in Germany my comrades of the Third International. I almost regained the jewels that belonged, not to any countess, her family, red with the blood of peasants, but to the people. If I had regained those stones they would have gone back to serve the Soviet; to help free the workers of the world, to buy the bombs that would blow up the capitalistic nations. Had I succeeded that priest would not have gone into my Russia, the Nazis would have rotted in jails, the Countess would have been stripped of her ill-gotten jewels and I should have returned to Moscow, from which I proudly come, an honoured man; a power in the party; a hero to my people.

But I failed. Still, I am like the other martyrs of human justice. To me blood was nothing if I could, through blood, reach my noble ends. Only I should like to know how they found out it was I. Knowing that, I think I should die happy for the cause that is mine, Stalin's, and the Third International's.

Chapter Nine

The little parlour of Fr. Tierney's rectory seemed uncommonly bright. In a mild way, the priest and his two friends—the organist and the detective—were having a kind of celebration. For on the morrow St. Sergius' Uniate Catholic Church would hold its first public service and the bishop himself had, in his usual gracious fashion, promised to attend in all his dignity. Because of the tragic events that had surrounded it, the church itself had become so famous that thousands who had never heard of the Greek Catholic Rite had flocked to see it and help the young priest, who regarded this little parish as a steppingstone to the days when he would carry the Faith back into the sad, godless Soviet.

So there was coffee on the table and cheese and crackers. And the men, completely relaxed, were threshing out the mystery that had come so close to wrecking the lives of two of them.

"From the start," said Reilly, "it was perfectly clear to me and to Karl here too—he's the real detective on this case—that the crime could have been committed only by someone very close to you, Fr. Tierney; someone who had almost the run of the house. He knew his way around the sacristy. He knew about that safe and the jewels. He was even in a position to steal your biretta and place it so that instant suspicion would fall on you. Now, if he wanted to do this sort of thing to a priest—quite aside from his wanting to steal the jewels—he must have either hated you, Fr. Tierney, personally or hated the priesthood as an institution, or hated what you were planning to do in the priesthood. I could find no one who hated you personally, so I looked for a Russian communist—a man who, with the jewels, would benefit personally or benefit a cause and at the same time bring you to disgrace."

"Only," said Fr. Tierney, "none of us knew of such a man."

"No, but Karl here and Radolf and Anton—his real name is of course not Anton; I doubt that we'll ever know what it is—were the only three who had the run of your house. Though Anton faked ignorance of the jewels, it was entirely possible that he knew of them. That biretta, instead of leading to you, led, I thought, away from you. And I confess that from the start neither of us even slightly considered you as a possible killer."

They all laughed at the absurdity of the idea, Fr. Tierney with a kind of wry relief. Reilly indicated Karl. "Karl here was with the dead man when Anton arrived in the sacristy. But where was Anton before then? He said he arrived in the church and went straight to the organ loft and sat down to wait. That was possible, but any man who had the run of your place could easily have done this. He could have arrived earlier than Karl, gone straight to the sacristy, begun to break the safe and been caught by Radolf; murdered Radolf, left the church by the rear door, locked the door, throwing the key into the ash pit. When Karl, who was in the choir loft, heard strange sounds and went to the sacristy, Anton could have returned to the choir loft."

Karl laughed. "Don't be too clever, Sergeant. We know that that's how Anton did it, but it was a long time before we suspected that that might have been the way. I confess that I began to suspect him only when I was in the church the night that someone was playing the organ. God gave me a remarkable memory for music. Play me a phrase and I'll remember it as long as I live.

"Well the night of the murder, Anton was in the choir loft when I was in the sacristy. People who have a slight musical ability and just a little knowledge of music usually play the same few chords every time they sit down at a piano, or any other keyboard. Anton knew a little music; just enough to play these chords. They stuck in my memory. When I went back to the church that night the person in the choir loft played the same chords. For once my memory went dry. I knew the chords but the events of that horrible murder had knocked the exact context of that music out of my mind. When I did remember, I had the key that opened all the doors. It was Anton who had played when I discovered the murder. It was Anton who played in an attempt to locate, once more, the exact spot in the organ where he had tossed the jewels. If some of the jewels hadn't hit that old pipe we might never have found the gems. At least not until in some future generation, that old organ was taken to the boneyard of departed musical instruments. But when on the night of the murder Anton heard that squeak, he knew he'd be able to locate the exact spot where the gems lay. That's why he played his familiar chords again in the dark church."

Reilly shook his head. "One chump thing he overlooked: once services were begun in the church, wouldn't the organ always squeak and give away the hiding place?"

Father Tierney laughed. "That is where his luck might have held, and he knew it too. We don't use an organ in the Greek Rite. We sing without organ. And if he could have persuaded Karl here to have choir practices at home…"

"That would have been luck," the detective agreed. They sipped their coffee thoughtfully.

"Meantime," said Karl, "let's give the Sergeant credit for an important stroke."

Reilly looked thoughtful. "That was luck too. If Lyndski hadn't decided to get himself involved in the case, I might never have thought of the Barrier Smoke Shop; except insofar as it concerned Mrs. Goodspeed and the Jap."

The priest held up his hand. "Now there's something that doesn't fit in. How in thunder did she happen to have those jewels? She wasn't near the scene of the murder, and that cock-and-bull story about receiving them through the mail…"

"Did you notice," said Reilly, "that the minute Senator Goodspeed mentioned his connection with the investigation of anti-American societies, I dropped his wife as a suspect. It was the most likely thing in the world to suppose that those he was attacking would want to strike back at him; and how better than through a gambling wife? But that's where Anton over-reached himself; he was a fool there as he was a fool in other instances. Somehow in the rush of hiding the jewels in the organ he found himself with that unset diamond and the ruby ring. He couldn't safely keep them so he decided to make things hot for one of his enemies and he did. He simple sent the ring and the stone through the mail to a desperate woman. She, another fool, saw in them a way of quietly paying her gambling debts. The Jap was a willing go-between, and the minute we spotted them, Senator Goodspeed was headed for scandal. Anton had struck at a man whose very existence was a menace to himself and his party. If he hadn't done that—" Reilly laughed, "No, there was Lyndski. Isn't it in *Pinafore* the little buttercup sings the song about things not always being what they seem?

Well, the Barrier Smoke Shop gets its money from the suckers, but back in the second room, the one that lies behind the records room we investigated, there's a spot from which communist propaganda pours out to the country—to unions, the army, the Great Lakes Naval Station, Fort Sheridan. Anton, according to his own story, used to drop in for little bets. He was on their books alright, but that personal business on which he used to slip away at intervals, took him to this Barrier Smoke Shop a lot oftener than would be necessary for an occasional two dollar on the nose. We know the real Reds of the city; Clineman is a Red of the reddest tinge, O'Rafity was run out of Ireland for anti-republican and anti-free-state activities. The Valera doesn't like the Reds any better than do most of the real democrats. Well, when I spotted that possible connection between Anton and the Reds there...

"Then Lyndski calls up, announces that he can tell us what we want to know, and is bumped off. Bumped off, please remember, while Anton is out of the place and could, if the humour seized him, do the job. I spent quite a bit of time with Clineman and O'Rafity, on and off, for the next few days for I couldn't see why Lyndski, a Red, should want to turn in a brother Red. Only I suddenly found out that Lyndski didn't regard any of them as brother Reds.

After his death we picked up the letters that he had received from Mexico. You know what that means?"

"Trotsky," said Fr. Tierney, who knew his Russian complications.

"And if a Nazi used to hate a communist, hasn't this recent fine clinch of Hitler and Stalin got us all muddled up? A Trotskyite hates a Stalinite as a Chinaman hates a Jap. Lyndski was preparing to talk to get Anton before Anton got him, but fortunately for him, Anton recognized Lyndski's over the phone and it was curtains for Lyndski. What's another man or two out of the way if it means that the great cause advances? So," said Fr. Tierney softly, "you had your communist, your priest hater. And he was right in the bosom of my parish!"

Neither of them liked to face what the priest was facing; treason, treachery, and hatred masking as friendship, so Reilly hurried on.

"That Lyndski situation really focused my attention on Anton; that, and the fact that never did tragic things happen in a time when he couldn't have been the doer. He could have been in the dark church that night—"

"I was worried, though," broke in Fr. Tierney, "when I heard that your Bund cap, Karl, had been the one found in the church that night you tracked down the man at the organ. Of course I was sure you weren't guilty, but would the public and eventually a jury believe that?"

Karl laughed. "In all my life," he admitted, "I was never more flabbergasted than when Schwartz held out the Bund cap we were so sure was his and announced emphatically that it was mine."

"My first reaction," said the sergeant "was the conviction that Schwartz was guilty. Either he had gotten hold of Karl's cap—"

"But how could he have?" interrupted Karl.

"—or knowing Karl's number in the Bund," continued Reilly, "he had prepared a new cap with that number and left it behind in the choir loft to throw the suspicion on Karl."

Karl cheesed his cracker. "Almost more than anything else," he seemed to be musing aloud, "the finding of that cap made me think of Anton. First of all the guilty man was likely to think the same way twice. He had thought of a biretta in the case of Fr. Tierney. He thought of a cap in my case. His mind ran to headpieces, so to speak. The Sergeant says he wondered whether Schwartz might not have stolen my cap? Conceivably. But I thought how easy it would have been for Anton, going and coming as he did in my quarters, to pick it up and carry it off. Besides, whoever the guilty man was, he had access to Fr. Tierney's quarters; otherwise he could not easily have got the biretta. He had easy access to my quarters; otherwise he could not easily have got the Bund cap. No one else fitted those circumstances, but Anton. Yes, almost more than anything else, that Bund cap flung my whole attention to Anton."

"And your aim," the sergeant nodded, "was remarkably accurate."

The priest raised a protest. "But what about the night watches? Why in the world didn't he get the jewels when he was alone in the church?"

"And have full suspicion pointed to him?" the detective laughed. "No, he went home and to bed. Then Karl here goes on duty and is consequently under the possibility of suspicion. And Karl is knocked out and there is evidence carefully left behind to prove that Karl knocked himself out—that was the brick and hammer trick."

"It would have fooled me," said the priest. "Fooled me to the hilt, only…"

"Right," said the detective, "you're positively warm. But there'd be this to consider; why should he work up an elaborate gag like that and then leave the evidence lying around for the detectives to pick up and pin right on him? All Karl had to do, if he had knocked himself out, was pick up the hammer and brick when he woke in the morning, hide them and stagger out. A clear case of assault. But when we found that brick and hammer, I just knew he didn't knock himself out."

Karl bowed in gratitude for this slight tribute to his brains.

"Yet," said the priest, "you staged this elaborate accusation of Karl, always in Anton's presence. And Karl escapes and leaves the detective tied up like a mummy."

"You tell him, Karl," said the detective.

"You remember that Reilly told us after the case broke that Anton had said regretfully that he couldn't stay in town and face life if you or I were guilty. That gave him his getaway story, so he packed the jewels into the suitcase and checked it at the New York Central station. It took the detectives only part of a morning to locate the suitcase. The initials P.A. and lightness of the practically empty suitcase were a perfect giveaway.

"But I had to seem so guilty that Pierre would be thrown completely off guard. You never in your life saw a more cooperative victim than the detective in the hospital room. He even showed me how to gag him! And don't you realize that in any well regulated hospital people would have been in and out of that room a dozen times in the interval that I was gone, if we hadn't set the stage?"

Fr. Tierney sighed. "But all the people dragged together like that—"

"To make Anton think he was the only one not suspected," finished Reilly. "I kept him in my confidence, took him along as my Dr. Watson, made him feel I trusted him to the hilt. Everyone was a possible culprit but him. Then when Karl arrived with the bag that headquarters furnished him and flashed it on Anton, he was so completely taken off his feet that he confessed with every look, gesture, flush, stammer, protest. He was caught, and because it was at the very moment that he was sure he'd escaped without a thought's being directed toward him, he was completely off balance and he fell, physically and mentally."

Fr. Tierney poured fresh coffee for them. "And that, believe me, is the last time I play custodian for anyone's money or jewels. The church was meant to be poor; I'll win Russia back to Christ anyway."

Karl sniffed indignantly. "At that, the Countess might have handed you half a dozen stones just out of gratitude! Why are rich people so often miserly?"

"That," remarked Reilly cynically, "is probably how they got rich."

But Fr. Tierney was shaking his head. "Once is enough. I'm glad she didn't give me a thing: its better that way. Let the banks take care of money and jewels. I'm custodian of the real treasures of the Church; the poor, the weak, the ignorant."

At this final decisive speech of Fr. Tierney's his guests rose to leave. They shook hands at the door of the rectory. Karl turned to gaze up at the sky where the moon was fighting its way through Chicago smoke and fog. Then he smiled at the priest. These harrowing days had drawn them very close together.

"You're not feeling you'd like to take a brief, brisk walk before you turn in, are you?" Karl asked.

The priest shook his head. "It's early to bed, for tomorrow I'm rising early."

They both looked their polite, but curious interest. "Yes," said the priest, "and you might say a little prayer for that too. I'm paying my second visit to Anton in his cell."

It was hard for the two others not to look the surprise they felt. But Fr. Tierney continued. "Once on a time, I'm sure, he had Faith and saw, beyond the universe, the Father who made the world out of love for men."

The sergeant almost blustered. "Not Anton! You're not wasting your time on Anton!"

"Not," supplemented Karl, "after the things he did to you."

Fr. Tierney's eyes grew almost mystic. "Why not? After all, Russia is so far away. Who knows whether I shall ever reach it? Maybe Anton is the whole reason why I am what I am." He moved his arms in a gesture that took in his cassock, the church, all that he had built up around himself. "Russia can wait, but Anton can't. And if before he mounts the scaffold I can show him what the love and forgiveness of Christ really are…"

They looked at the priest with something like awe. "Good night, my friends," he clasped their hands again. Then, in the strange, old-world phrase, "Go with God, and may He keep you all your days and all your ways," he watched them as they walked silently down the street.

Had they followed him into his little church where that day Eucharistic Christ had for the first time taken up his dwelling, their hope for Pierre Anton, strangely reborn, would have grown even stronger and more secure.

The End

www.ingramcontent.com/pod-product-compliance
Ingram Content Group UK Ltd.
Pitfield, Milton Keynes, MK11 3LW, UK
UKHW041928190726
13854UKWH00004B/1512